GET MORE OF MY BOOKS FREE!

To say thank you for buying this book, I'd like to invite you to my exclusive *VIP Club*, and give you some of my books and short stories for FREE.

To join the club, head to **adamcroft.net/vip-club** and two free books will be sent to you straight away! And the best thing is it won't cost you a penny — ever.

Adam Croft

For more information, visit my website: **adamcroft.net**

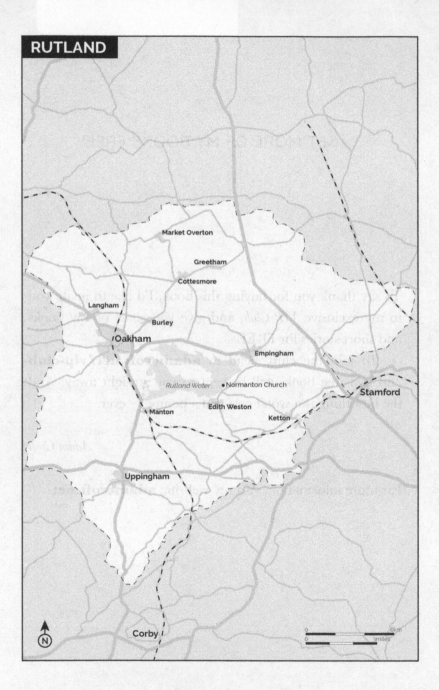

RUTLAND

Market Overton

Greetham

Cottesmore

Langham

Burley

Oakham

Empingham

Rutland Water • Normanton Church

Stamford

Manton

Edith Weston

Ketton

Uppingham

Corby

N

WHAT LIES BENEATH

ADAM CROFT

OAKHAM

Ashwell Road

Burley Road

Rutland Police

Oakham
Station

Cold Overton Road

West Road

High Street

Stamford Road

Uppingham Road

N

0

0   1km

1mile

For Bob Tranter, Sunday mornings began the moment they shut off the outboard motor. The only sounds left were those of the birds, the lapping of the water and the odd car in the distance. This was his heaven.

He rolled with the movement of the boat as his friend, Geoff Hampson, unzipped the Thermos bag and took out their supplies: a Cornish pasty each (still warm) and a flask of black coffee to share. To Bob and Geoff, it was what Sundays were all about.

Each week, Bob set his Sunday alarm for seven o'clock. Then it was straight into the shower and dressed ready for half past, when Geoff would pull up outside Bob's house in Corby — bumping his way up the kerb as he always did — ready to arrive at the Rutland Water Fishing Lodge just before eight. There was something special about being the first boat out.

It wasn't always fishing, of course. Sometimes they'd happily bob around on the water all morning, or occasionally head over towards Egleton or Barnsdale to spot birds. Either way, it was the ultimate form of relaxation. As much as they loved their wives, there was nothing more enjoyable than spending a few hours on Rutland Water, alone in a boat and putting the world to rights.

Bob sank his teeth into the thick pastry, his tastebuds coming alive as he devoured the snack within seconds. Each week he told himself he'd make the next one last longer, and each week the hunger took control.

He sniffed as he unscrewed the top of the Thermos flask and poured himself a cup of coffee, watching as the steam rose upwards, swirling amongst the morning mist, becoming one with it.

'Beautiful morning for it,' he said, the same as he did each week, whatever the weather.

'You're not wrong there,' Geoff replied, true to the script.

Bob sniffed again. 'Much new with you, then?'

'Nothing to write home about. You?'

'Nah. Same old, same old. You know how it is.'

'That I do, Bob. That I do.'

Today wasn't a fishing day — that much had been decided the night before, when Geoff had called Bob to confirm he was still on for a seven-thirty pick-up. That was part of the routine, too. A seemingly pointless cog in the machine of their Sunday morning relaxation. It had been the same for years. It was comfortable, familiar. Today was for 'just sitting'. Their annual permit gave them the right to fish, but there was no law saying they had to, and no-one had told them off yet. Besides, 'just sitting' shook things up occasionally. It was an exciting divergence from what would otherwise be boring and routine.

'Good pasty?' Geoff asked, in case Ginsters had radically changed their recipe since last week.

'Beautiful.'

'Not bad, are they?'

'Not bad at all, Geoff. Not bad at all.'

Bob had tried to explain the fascination to Freda, but she didn't understand. She said it sounded boring floating around in a wooden hull for hours on end, doing nothing, talking about nothing. Which was odd, considering how damned good Freda was at talking endlessly about nothing at all.

The nothingness was precisely the point. Out here on the water, there were no stresses. He wasn't being nagged. He didn't have to spend two hours on hold trying to get through to Legal & General to sort out his contents insurance. He didn't have to listen to Mrs Calderwood's sodding dog barking all day. He was only half an hour from home, but he might as well have been in paradise.

'Here, wassat?' Geoff said, deviating from the script.

'Where?'

'Over there, on the rocks.'

'Can't see from here,' Bob replied. 'Left me glasses in the car.'

'You and me both. Start her up, will you? We'll go have a looksee. Something's not right, here.'

Bob had to agree. They knew the water like the backs of their hands, and this was far from normal.

With the outboard motor spluttering to life, the boat

made its way towards the rocks at Normanton Church. Bob squinted as they neared, trying to make out the shapes. To him, it looked as though someone had dumped a big bag or a pile of clothes on the rocks. But as they got closer, it became immediately apparent to Bob that this was no pile of clothes.

He sucked in a breath. Adrenaline bolted through his chest.

'Bugger me,' he said. 'It's a body.'

Caroline Hills had her own Sunday routine, albeit a much simpler one: pancakes.

She wasn't a stickler for routine, but the sizzle of batter in a frying pan on Sunday mornings was one stitch that connected her family with their previous life in London. And it was a good stitch; not like those rotten, frayed ones which had needed pulling out.

Rutland seemed a million miles from Cricklewood, and that was no bad thing. London was a past life — one which was best left alone.

'Tea?' Mark asked, placing one hand on the small of her back as he kissed her on the cheek.

'Coffee, please. Black.'

'Ooh. One of those?'

'Didn't sleep well. Kept tossing and turning.'

Mark forced a smile. 'Ah. I slept like a log. Sorry.'

'I noticed,' she said, smiling.

'Listen, I was going to suggest we all go for a walk or a

bike ride later. It's meant to be a nice day, once the mist clears. Will do the boys the world of good, too. Get them off that bloody Xbox for a couple of hours.'

She couldn't argue with that. Josh was as addicted to console games as any other ten-year-old. But it was the frequency with which six-year-old Archie played them that worried her most. Back in London, it hadn't been an issue. The odd game of FIFA or Fortnite was preferable to the boys walking the streets of Cricklewood and Neasden. But Rutland was a different world altogether, and she knew it'd be good for the boys to get out and about a bit more.

Caroline remembered how her husband's eyes had lit up when he'd found out about Rutland's cycling and leisure scene. He'd always cycled when they'd lived in London and was a fitness fanatic. Try as she might, she couldn't think of anything she'd rather do less.

'Yeah, maybe,' she said. 'Let's see how the weather turns out.'

'I was thinking we could even pop into a village pub somewhere, get to know a few of the locals.'

Caroline raised an eyebrow.

'It'd be good to make some contacts,' he said. 'Friends, even. It's a pretty sociable place, and I feel like we should at least try to join in. I still can't get used to people saying hello when you walk past them in the street.' Mark stirred the mug of instant coffee and handed it to her. 'It'll be good for the boys,' he said.

'Yeah, you're probably right. Let's wait for it to warm up a bit first, though, eh? I haven't quite acclimatised enough to have stocked up on jodhpurs and waxed jackets yet.'

'Ooh arr, you're a local now, missus!' Mark teased, embarrassing himself with a faux West Country accent rather than the gentle East Midlands burr of the local area.

Caroline shook her head and laughed before turning back towards the stove and flipping the gently sizzling pancakes.

'Nearly ready?' Mark asked.

'Almost.'

'Boys, grub's up!' he yelled, without taking even a cursory step towards the bottom of the stairs.

Seconds later came the sound of feet thundering down the staircase, before two hungry faces — complete with bed-head hair — arrived in the kitchen.

'I hope you two are hungry,' Caroline said. 'I think I've done too much batter.'

'Extra energy for the cycle ride,' Mark added.

'Are we going for a bike ride?' Archie asked.

'Maybe. We'll see what the weather does,' Caroline said.

'Doesn't look brilliant from here,' Josh mumbled, another sign of becoming a teenager long before his time.

'My app says the mist'll clear by ten,' Mark said, playing with his phone. 'It's meant to get up to twenty degrees after that.'

'And in old money?' Caroline asked, sliding three pancakes onto separate plates. With only three frying pans, she always made sure the family ate first. She'd have whatever was left.

'Sixty-eight,' Mark said.

Caroline smiled a little and nodded. Perhaps it wasn't going to be such a bad day after all.

As she poured more batter into the pans, she noticed the sound of her work phone vibrating on the table in the hall.

'Ah, can you grab that for me?' she said, not noticing that Mark was already making his way out of the kitchen to do so. He returned a few seconds later and handed the phone to her.

When she saw Dexter Antoine's name on the screen, she had a feeling it wasn't going to be good news.

'Dex, what's up?' she said, answering the call.

'Morning. Sorry, but I hope you didn't have plans for today.'

'Uh, well sort of,' she said, looking at Mark. 'Why?'

'Someone's found a body on the water over at Normanton. Looks like murder. Do you want me to phone it through to the boys at EMSOU?'

Caroline knew when she took the job as the sole Detective Inspector of Rutland Police that it was usual practice for homicides and other major and violent crimes to be handed to the regional East Midlands Special Operations Unit. Whereas they had a dedicated major crime unit, Rutland Police was by far the smallest force in the entire country.

Rutland itself was barely sixteen by eighteen miles in size and the smallest historic county in England, with fewer than forty-thousand inhabitants. It was what had appealed most to Caroline when she'd decided to escape the Met. As much as she'd enjoyed the change of pace, it had been a huge shift for her.

In the Met, she'd known her place. There were plenty of large investigations for her to get her teeth into and prove herself. Here, though, things had been different. She'd seen the capabilities of her team, but she hadn't yet had the chance to show them what she was made of.

'No,' she said, not even needing to think about her answer. 'No, we'll take it.'

There was a moment of silence at the other end of the phone. 'Are you sure? First responders seemed pretty sure we're looking at murder.'

'Yes, I'm sure. It's my patch, and official procedure is that cases are only handed over on my say-so. And I'm not saying so.'

'Well, if you're sure. It'd probably be good to come down and have a look first, then we can decide what to do.'

'Dex, I'm not handing it over. Text me the postcode, will you?'

There was another moment of silence. 'Well, it's Normanton Church. You've heard of it, right?'

'Yeah, course. But I don't want to get lost on the way. Just easier to stick it into the satnav, isn't it? What's the postcode?'

'Uh, I'm not really sure it has one. I can look.'

Caroline sighed. 'Don't worry. I'll find it. Meet me there.'

3

Just over a quarter of an hour later, Caroline had parked up in the nearest access car park to the church. It would leave her with a short walk along the front of the water, from the fishing lodge where she'd parked, to the Normanton Church causeway. Although she was a city girl at heart, she could see the appeal of being down here early on a Sunday morning.

DS Antoine was waiting for her at the end of the causeway that led to Normanton Church.

'Morning, Dex,' she said, as if she'd just walked into the office to find him at his desk. 'Not a bad little spot, this. I never knew it was here.'

'You do surprise me,' Dexter replied with a wry smile.

'Detective Inspector Hills,' she said, flashing her ID badge at the uniformed constables who were manning the outer cordon. 'So what have we got?'

'Down here,' Dexter said, leading Caroline towards the church. As they approached, she noticed that something didn't quite look right. The church was low, almost as if half of it was underground. It appeared to be floating on the water. 'Over here on the rocks. Ligature marks on the neck, possibly consistent with strangulation, and some sort of blunt force wound on the back of his head. I reckon that's what finished him off. But look how he's laid out. Bizarre, eh?'

Caroline took in the scene in front of her. The church jutted out onto Rutland Water on its own private stone jetty, surrounded on all sides by huge boulders, which sloped down towards the lapping water. The body — that of a man — lay face down on the rocks, his arms outstretched, legs straight.

'What you thinking?' Dexter asked.

'Probably what you're thinking, I imagine. There's no way the water's washed him up here. It's too neat. He's been laid out in a crucifixion pose. Besides which, he's almost bone dry, apart from his legs.'

The man's feet were under the water, which lapped up at his lower legs, the bottom half of his trousers sodden.

'It's weird. Kinda looks like he's just crawled out of the water like some sort of zombie.'

'Yes, Dex. That's what we've got here. A zombie apocalypse.'

Dexter looked at her. 'You serious?'

'No. I think he's been put there. That begs the question why. Why go to the trouble of doing that? Why not hide the body? Bury it, even? And then there's the logistics. You can't get a car down here, so the killer will've had to have used a wheelbarrow or something. Dead bodies are heavier than you think. There's no way he was carried. That's a huge amount of effort to go to, when it'd be easier to just dig a hole somewhere and chuck him in. This is deliberate.'

Dexter shuffled uncomfortably. 'A message of some sort?'

'Possibly. Look at the symbolism. Crucifixion pose, right in front of the church. And if I'm not mistaken…' she said, walking back towards the church and peering in through the low windows, 'yep, he's facing the altar. I doubt it's a coincidence the killer's put him in that exact place. And, as my rumbling stomach has just reminded me, it's a Sunday morning.'

'Mmmm. Maybe. Only one problem with that.'

Caroline looked at him, waiting for his explanation.

'It's not technically a church. Hasn't been for decades. It was deconsecrated years back.'

'Deconsecrated?'

'Long story. I'll fill you in on the details when we get back to the office.'

Caroline smiled. 'Quite the fount of local knowledge, aren't you?'

'Yeah, sometimes. Not exactly the busiest job, being a detective in Rutland, so I like to familiarise myself with the area and its history, yeah.'

'Good. Well, hopefully that'll come in useful. We'll need to look more into the history of this place. Doesn't look to me as if it's been picked at random. Do we have ID on him yet?'

'Not at the moment. Waiting on the SOCOs before we start going through pockets. Don't much fancy chancing those rocks, either. Uniform leant over to check for a pulse, and even she nearly lost her footing a couple of times.'

'Who found the body?'

'Two old boys over there,' Dexter said, nodding his head in the direction of a bench near the main footpath. 'They were out on a boat. Must've been a shock.'

Caroline looked down at the body on the rocks and thought about the family who were about to find out they'd just lost a loved one. 'Yes. Yes, I imagine it was.'

4

With the area secured and handed over to the scenes of crime and forensics officers, Caroline and Dexter took Bob and Geoff along the path to the main car park by the fishing lodge. They sat down at a table in the glass-fronted Waterside Cafe, overlooking the water.

'DS Antoine is going to take some notes, as well as recording this on his phone. Is that okay with you both?' Caroline asked.

Bob and Geoff nodded, neither of them having said a word since she'd suggested they sit down somewhere warm to chat.

On any other day, their position would've given them a superb view of the fishing boats going out, one every few seconds, as the vast expanse of Rutland Water opened up in front of them. Now, though, there was nothing. The boats remained moored up against the jetty, the water off limits for the foreseeable future.

'Can you talk me through what happened this morning, please?' Caroline asked, directing her question at Bob. 'From the beginning.'

'Well, we arrived here just before eight. That's when it opens, see. We like to try and get a full day of it if we can. Not much else doing. Geoff picks me up about half seven and we come straight here.'

'Did you come by car?'

'Yeah.'

'Where did you park?'

'Right outside here, in the car park we just walked through.'

'So you didn't get a view of the church until you were out on the water?'

'No, love. Not really. In any case, you're hardly on the look out for dead bodies, are you? See the odd fish that's carked it, if the birds haven't already had it. That's about it. Never a human.'

This struck Caroline as an odd way to describe the situation, but she let it fly. 'So whereabouts were you when you first saw the body?'

'Well, when we first saw it *were* a body, we was pretty much on top of it. But Geoff spotted there were something there.'

'Where were you?' Caroline asked again.

'Out on the water.'

'Whereabouts?'

'Well, I dunno. Not many signposts out there, you know what I mean?'

Geoff cut in. 'Probably about a third of the way to the Hambleton peninsula. In line with the fishing lodge, I'd say. We hadn't headed in either direction at that point.'

'So that's, what, about three or four hundred metres from the church?'

Geoff shrugged. 'If you say so. Close enough to see something out the ordinary, but far enough away not to know what it was.'

Caroline felt like she was spinning round in circles. 'And you say you only realised it was a body when you were quite close?'

'Yeah. Close as we could get without worrying about beaching it, anyway. Don't tend to bother wearing our glasses out on the water, see. Not really a whole lot of point. Not unless we're bird watching.'

'And you didn't recognise the person?'

'Not from the back of his head, no.'

'So what did you do?'

'I phoned you lot. Bob steered us over to the bank by the main footpath, 'cos we didn't know how shallow the rocks got. Figured we had to moor up quick, and soil seemed a better bet than rocks.'

'Tenner says they charge us for that at the lodge,' Bob said, interjecting. 'Not meant to do that, you're not.'

Caroline forced a smile. 'I think they've probably got bigger things to worry about at the moment. Did either of you see anyone else by the church, or on that area of the water? Either before or after?'

The pair shook their heads. 'No, no-one,' Bob said. 'We

was the first ones out on the water. We like to be, see. Didn't see no-one else over that way. Occasionally see the odd dog walker or jogger on the footpath, but very quiet this morning. Probably the mist. Don't get many people out until that clears, usually.'

It struck Caroline that there wasn't a whole lot she was going to get out of Bob and Geoff. She gave Dexter a knowing look, took their contact details and thanked them for their time.

As they stood to leave, a man — who Caroline estimated was in his mid to late sixties and who was wearing a knitted jumper with a bizarre frog pattern — approached them with a polystyrene mug of tea in his hand.

'Terrible business, that. You're the police, I presume?'

'We are, yes,' Dexter said. 'And you are?'

'Oh, sorry,' the man replied, shuffling the tea into his left hand and extending his right. 'Howard Smallwood. I've lived round here all my life and I've never seen anything like this before. Makes you wonder what the world's coming to, doesn't it?'

'Indeed,' Caroline said, smiling and starting to walk away.

'If you need anything, by the way, I might be able to help. I'm the president of the local history society. I know all the little nooks and crannies, not to mention most of the people round here. If I can help you join any dots, just give me a shout!'

The man handed each of them a cheap business card with his details on. Caroline gave another smile, inwardly pleased that even in the midst of a violent murder, Rutland still had its eccentric characters to offer.

The air was already warming by the time she and Dexter stepped back outside and into the car park. It was shaping up to be a beautiful day. For one family, though, things were about to get a whole lot darker.

5

Caroline was thankful she'd managed to get this far without any serious pressure to hand the case over to EMSOU, the East Midlands Special Operations Unit. She knew that time would come, so for now her priority was to get her investigation up and running as quickly and smoothly as possible. She was determined to show she was up to the task, and that her tiny CID unit was capable of handling more than the odd case of fraud or burglary.

There was one thing she couldn't change, though. Resources. Rutland had by far the smallest police force in the country, by virtue of being the smallest ceremonial county and it enjoyed an historically low crime rate. Even with their tiny numbers, they were rarely swamped with work. It was usual for a murder investigation to consist of dozens of specially trained officers at EMSOU. So when such an event came along in Rutland, it was extraordinarily rare for it to be dealt with 'in house'. That made Caroline even more determined to prove her worth.

Although she was a Detective Inspector, her day-to-day duties tended to cross over quite substantially with uniform. It was an odd setup, but one she'd come to respect and enjoy in her short time in the job. There was something safe in the mundanity of ensuring resources were deployed properly, setting and assessing key performance indicators or identifying and managing local threats. But she couldn't deny it lacked the excitement and exhilaration of a murder case. And this would be her first since leaving the Met.

She'd always intended to take full control when — if — that first murder case crossed her desk. Although convention dictated handing it over to EMSOU, it was far from a written rule. It was more a recommendation for reasons of expediency, and because it was deemed impossible for her small team to deal with something that big. Caroline, though, knew that the size of a team rarely mattered. From her experience in the Met, bloated teams often moved more slowly. There was a certain diligence in smaller units — a sense of deep personal responsibility. Besides which, the decisive breakthrough in any case tended to come from a discovery made by one sharp-eyed officer, and was not usually dictated by the size of the team.

They'd all be working long hours. Annual leave would be a distant memory. But Caroline was determined to lead from the front. She needed to — even if the thought gave her a flicker of doubt and a twinge of nausea.

With her team assembled in front of her, she opened the first of her morning briefings on Operation Forelock — the name that had been chosen by the Police National Computer from a pre-approved list of 'neutral' words. She watched the officers as she reeled off the familiar pre-amble — familiar to her, at least — and noticed an atmosphere of keen anxiety that seemed to be shared by everyone. They recognised the magnitude of the situation and were keen to do all they could to manage it to the best of their abilities. Caroline knew major cases were what tended to show either the strength in a team or expose its cracks, and she hoped Operation Forelock would provide her with the former rather than the latter.

'First things first, I believe we have an identity on the victim. DS Antoine?'

'That's right. His name's Roger Clifton, sixty years old. He's a local businessman. Lived in Rutland all his life. He's been on and off the local council for years.'

'He's well-known locally, then?' Caroline asked.

'Enough for one of the forensics boys to have recognised him as soon as he turned up to the scene.'

Caroline smiled inwardly. *How very Rutland*, she thought. 'So what's the situation? Is he popular?'

Dexter shuffled awkwardly. 'Like I say, he's been on and off the council for years.'

A ripple of laughter rumbled around the room.

'Alright, I think I get it,' Caroline said. 'What line of business is he in?'

'Construction,' Dexter replied, the hint of a smile on his face.

'Ah. I think I see the connection here. Would I be right in presuming there's a correlation between his spells on the council and his involvement in local construction projects?'

'Not for me to say, boss. Got to be worth looking into, though.'

'I'd say so. We'll need to speak to his colleagues, too. Let's have a look into the setup of his company, see what's going on there. We might struggle today with it being a Sunday, but let's see what we can do. What else is there?'

'The company's based in Burley. Arthur Clifton Construction, it's called.'

'Arthur?'

'His grandad, according to the company's website. He was the original owner, and it's since been passed down to Roger.'

'If Roger's sixty, Arthur must be long gone by now. There's a good chance his dad, Arthur's son, will be too. Any living family that we know of?'

'His wife and daughter live in Empingham. On paper, so does he, but what we're hearing is they're not exactly a conventional couple. He "works away a lot", apparently.'

'Lovely. Nice and simple from the outset, then.'

'I'll put a few feelers out, see if we can get to the bottom of what's going on there,' Sara Henshaw said. Sara was a young DC who'd initially made her mark as the community liaison officer for Oakham. She'd lived in the town her whole life, and her innovative and engaging use of the Oakham Community Policing Team's social media account had drawn plaudits both locally and beyond. Caroline knew Sara would be key to getting under the fabric of what had led to Roger Clifton's death.

'Actually, Sara, can you put out a call for witnesses? Social media, local radio, the lot. There's no way we've got the staff numbers for door-to-door just yet, so we need to get whatever we can.'

Sara nodded and wrote something down on her notepad. 'To be honest, no-one lives round Normanton anyway, so door-to-door enquiries wouldn't be much use. I'll speak to the staff at the Normanton Park Hotel — that's just next door. Other than that, by the time you see a residential property you're in Edith Weston.'

'Alright. See if there's any registered CCTV in the area, too. The hotel's probably a good bet. Try the fishing lodge as well, and any other business premises round there. If that doesn't bring anything up, look at residential. Might be worth a wander down the main road in Edith Weston. Might be someone who's got a camera pointing at the street and recording in higher resolution than a postage stamp. Unlikely, but worth a shot.'

'Boss, I think we've probably got to assume it was dark when the body was put there,' Dexter said. 'It's wide open down there. The church can be seen from the North Shore pretty easily. If you've got a pair of binoculars, you can even get a clear view from Egleton. And then there's pretty much the entire of the Hambleton peninsula.'

Rutland Water was more than three thousand acres in size and shaped like a horseshoe, the village of Upper Hambleton standing proudly on the peninsula, accessible only from the west, along a service road which met the A606 on the outskirts of Oakham. Although the tip of the Hambleton peninsula was barely five hundred metres from Normanton Church, getting there via dry land meant an almost eleven-mile, twenty-minute drive back along the peninsula and around the outside of Rutland Water.

'If it was dark,' Dexter continued, 'someone in the know could drive pretty much right up to the church. It's pitch black down there at night.'

'If that's the case, we're looking at someone involved with the church or the upkeep of the area, because I'm told the gates are locked up at night.'

'Is it possible the body wasn't dumped there, but was washed up from elsewhere? It could've been put in the water at a far more remote spot,' Sara Henshaw said.

Caroline shook her head. 'No chance. I saw the body. It was too fresh. It would've sunk before it reached Normanton, and only floated later. And from the way it was laid out on the rocks, I just can't see it. It was almost perfectly arranged. Not to mention bone dry. Tell me it's a coincidence that a body just happened to be left on the rocks outside the church on a Sunday morning, in full crucifixion pose, facing the altar.'

Much to Caroline's expectation, no-one challenged that point.

'So,' she said, changing the subject, 'we need to see who we can speak to. Find out who his fellow councillors are. See if there were any disagreements on that front, who his enemies were, who would've wanted him dead. Get onto his phone records. Aidan, can you get phone triangulation on his last known movements, please? We need to find out where he went and how he got there. Let's get a list of those colleagues at the construction company, too.' Aidan Chilcott was quiet, but diligent. Ever since she'd arrived in Rutland,

Caroline had strongly suspected Aidan had a thing for Sara, but that was something everyone else seemed completely oblivious to.

'Sara, find out the wife's plans,' she said. 'We'll need to speak to her, too.'

'Alright,' Dexter said. 'We'll get right onto it.'

'No you won't,' Caroline replied, picking up her notebook. 'You're coming with me.'

6

Caroline led Dexter through to her office — in reality, a poorly-partitioned corner of the room, whose door rattled every time anyone walked past or opened the main CID suite door — and sat down at her desk.

'Something the matter?' he asked her, confused by her brusque tone at the end of the morning briefing.

'No, why?'

'Just wondered. You wanted to see me?'

'Yes, take a seat. You're making the place look untidy. I wanted to find out a bit more about the local area. You mentioned it was a bit of a hobby of yours, local history and whatnot.'

'Got a bit of a passion brewing for local history, boss?' Dexter said, smiling.

'Not in the slightest,' Caroline said, laughing. 'But there could be a link with our man, and I want all angles covered. You said the church had been deconsecrated?'

'Yeah. Early seventies, I think.'

'I see. Tell me more.'

'Well, you know about how Rutland Water was formed, right?'

She'd heard one or two people mention it in the time she'd lived in the area, but the details had been lost on her.

'I think so. Remind me.'

'Well, up until the early seventies, it wasn't there. It was a valley with a few villages and hamlets in it. Then the water company came along and said they wanted to dam it and fill it up to create a new reservoir. There was a massive hoo-hah at the time, but it all went ahead. A lot of people lost their homes. To this day there are still two villages under Rutland Water. The Hambletons.'

'Isn't that on the peninsula?'

'Upper Hambleton is. Most people just call it Hambleton now because it's the only one left. Nether Hambleton and most of Middle Hambleton are under the water.'

'And what's that got to do with Normanton Church?'

'Ah, see that was meant to go as well. They cleared the valley for the reservoir, and the church was on the list. It was deconsecrated and marked for demolition, but there was a public outcry and they managed to save it. Only problem was, when the water was at its highest, it'd be halfway up the church walls and it'd be pretty much constantly flooded, so the rock barrier was built around it to keep the water away. They even filled the lower half of the church with concrete and made a new, higher floor. If you go in there now, it's weird. The windows are all really low and the ceiling's nowhere near the height of a normal church. From the outside it looks like it's sunk or is floating on the water, and when you're inside it's like being in Lilliput.'

'Blimey, Dex. Didn't realise you had such a literary bent. Wouldn't have had you down as a Dickens man.'

'Jonathan Swift, boss.'

'Hmm?'

'Gulliver's Travels. It was Jonathan Swift.'

Caroline shook her head and smiled. 'Well, well. Aren't you a box of surprises?'

'When you grow up in a house with three sisters hogging the bathroom and playing loud music, escaping into books seems pretty appealing. Especially when your dad's an English Literature professor.'

'Seriously? You kept that quiet,' Caroline said, internally admonishing herself for assuming a black kid from an estate in Leicester wouldn't be a reader of classics.

'Yeah, seriously. Only at De Montfort, mind, but still.'

Caroline laughed. She wasn't one for having work colleagues become friends, but even she had to admit she was becoming rather fond of Dexter Antoine.

Before Caroline left work later that day, Dexter pointed out that a few of them were going to the pub after work and asked her if she'd like to join them.

'It's only at the Wheatsheaf,' he said. 'Not really got to go far.'

It took Caroline a moment to place the pub — it seemed that every other pub in Rutland was called the Wheatsheaf — but all she wanted was to go home and curl up in bed.

'I'll pass if that's alright,' she said. 'But thanks for the offer.'

Dexter seemed to recognise there was no point in protesting, so he didn't.

When Caroline got home, Mark was waiting in the kitchen with a bottle of wine, pouring her a large glass as he heard her open the front door.

'Good day?' he asked, aware that she'd been called out on a major incident but without any information as to what had happened.

'Not sure that's the word I'd use,' Caroline said, eyeing the wine glass with unease.

'Big one?'

'Looks like it. A murder.'

Mark raised an eyebrow. Although he didn't work for the police, he knew what the expected procedure was, and he also knew how his wife would react to that. 'I don't suppose I need to ask if you're taking it on or handing it over, do I?'

'Why would I hand it over? I'm the on-call DI, I'm the assigned Senior Investigating Officer, I've got a brilliant team of detectives and — above all else — it's on my patch. What's the point of Rutland even having a police force if it's just going to roll over and phone EMSOU whenever there's anything trickier than a lost cat?'

Mark put his arms around her and kissed her on the forehead. 'I knew the answer already. There was never any doubt in my mind. Just like there's no doubt in my mind that what you need right now is that large glass of red.'

Caroline looked at the wine. 'Thanks, but I don't think that'll help. I need a clear head for work.'

'One won't hurt. They won't call you out again until tomorrow. They can't. And if they do, everything's walkable. I was thinking we could sit down and watch a film or something. We kind of lost our Sunday. Not complaining, by the way. Just thought it might be nice to spend the evening together, at least.'

'I know, but honestly, I'm knackered. I'd love to, but all I want to do is curl up in bed.'

'It's still early. You can at least stay up for an hour or so. You need to unwind anyway. It won't do you any good to go to bed while you're still stressed.'

She knew he needed the closeness right now — even if she felt dead on her feet. She picked up the glass and sniffed the wine. It smelled like vinegar. In that instant, she regretted letting Mark do the shopping last week.

'You know, that off-licence on Mill Street's pretty good. They've got some decent wines in there,' she said, as tactfully as she could.

'Yeah, I know. That's where I got this one.'

'Really?'

'Yeah. What's wrong with it?'

Caroline forced a smile, before taking a sip and swallowing it, doing her best to hide her natural reaction. 'Nothing,' she said, rubbing his arm. 'It's lovely.'

Fifteen minutes later, Caroline and Mark were sitting on the sofa in their living room. Mark had lit a couple of candles and put on a romcom film he thought Caroline might enjoy. But as he looked over at his wife, he could see she'd already fallen asleep.

7

The gentle buzzing of the phone alarm wrenched Caroline from her sleep, and she rolled over and looked at her bedside clock. Unfortunately, the alarm was right yet again. It was time to get up.

She blinked a few times as she recalled the previous evening. She didn't remember coming up to bed. The last thing in her memory was sitting down in front of the TV with a glass of wine that smelled like vinegar.

She got up, put on her clothes and went downstairs. Mark was in the kitchen getting the kids' stuff ready for school while they ate their breakfast.

'Morning,' he said, noticing her come in. 'Sleep well?'

'I think so, yeah. You?'

'You were dead to the world last night. Didn't even wake up when I carried you upstairs.'

'You carried me up?'

Mark laughed. 'Just about. Thought I was going to drop

you at one point. You mumbled something about a flood, then started snoring again.'

'Sorry.'

'Don't be. You clearly needed the sleep. Listen, I'll walk the boys to school. You take the extra time to wake yourself up.'

Caroline smiled and kissed her husband. He had an uncanny way of knowing when she needed him to step up to the plate. She watched as Josh quietly ate his cereal, hyper alert to any early-morning anxiety that might show on his face. He'd improved immeasurably since the move to Rutland, each of the family able to put their London troubles behind them, but she knew she would always be extra vigilant when it came to her eldest son. The bullying he'd suffered at his Cricklewood comprehensive would, she knew, cause him long-term damage. There was no doubting he was a different boy now. Quieter. More private. More reserved. She silently grieved his lost innocence and the carefree charm he'd always exuded, but which now lived on through his younger brother.

Archie was blissfully oblivious to all that had gone on. To him, this was an adventure. Caroline loved Archie's outlook on life, and wished it was one she could have herself. But what was most painful was that this had been Josh just a couple of years earlier. She'd fight with every bone in her body to make sure Archie didn't lose his innocence in the same way.

Once Mark had left to take the boys to school, Caroline gathered her stuff and decided to head straight to work.

There didn't seem much point hanging around an empty house, and in any case there'd be plenty for her to do once she got in.

The police station on Station Road — named for the trains, rather than the police — was only a ten-minute walk from home, but she could drive it in five. She still hadn't got over the novelty of being able to drive somewhere quicker than she could walk it. In London, that was almost unheard of. Besides, she didn't feel like walking today. She hadn't felt like walking any other day either, but she felt sure her time would come.

She climbed into her car, backed out onto the street and headed towards town.

Although most of Oakham's population knew the location of one police station next to the council offices on Catmos Street, many were unaware it was only really an enquiry desk and that the main police office was tucked away on Station Road, behind and within the grounds of Oakham School. In true austerity style, the original police building had been sold to the private school, and the current police office had been built on its own former car park.

The town was heaving with students, which charged boarders more than £11,000 a term, and whose campus was spread across all corners of Oakham. Caroline waited patiently with her indicator on until a group of students noticed her and waited for her to pull across the footpath and into the grounds of the police station.

The difference between her last workplace and this one could not have been starker. Caroline had been used to modern glass buildings and tower blocks in her time with the Met, and now she was working in a glorified hut in a school car park. If anything, for her it highlighted the continuity and immovability of policing. Two completely different locations, but much the same job.

'Morning, Dex,' she said as she opened the door to the CID suite and headed for her office. 'No-one else in yet?'

'Not yet. Still early, though. And there might be traffic.' Caroline raised an eyebrow. These people didn't know traffic. The closest she'd seen to rush hour carnage in Rutland was a queue of three cars waiting to cross the railway line while the barriers were down. 'Although, if you've got a couple of minutes, I've been doing some research. A couple of things which might be of interest.'

Caroline went over to Dexter's workstation, tugging a chair along with her, and sat down beside him.

'Right, so I've been digging deeper into the history. I think you're right. This is symbolic in some way. The church, the crucifixion pose, the Sunday morning. But I don't think it's a religious thing. I think it's a history thing.'

'Go on.'

'So the church isn't a church anymore, right? That kind of wipes out the religious aspect in my mind. There are a ton of churches in Rutland, and loads of them are pretty isolated at night so it'd be much easier to dump a body at one of those. Our killer, though, chose this location. Even though it's bloody impossible to get into overnight and it's a tourist hotspot. They went to a lot of effort. That tells me this place is symbolic. I think the choice of location and the crucifixion pose, the timing — all that — was symbolic of what this place *was* rather than what it *is*.'

Caroline blinked a couple of times. 'Right. Now bear in mind I've only had two cups of coffee this morning.'

Dexter smiled. 'And you're getting on a bit.'

Caroline laughed. 'Piss off. Now, tell me in English.'

'Alright, so basically I think we need to look more closely at the history. There's a ton of it round that area. The lost villages, the deliberate flooding, the public opposition, deconsecrating and saving the church, all of that. It totally divided opinion back then. I think it's probably safe to say it's been good for the area in the long run because it's brought tourism and stuff, but there's still a generation of people who are a bit sore about it all.'

'Wasn't this in the early seventies?' Caroline asked.

'Late sixties, early seventies, yeah.'

'That's fifty years ago. If we're looking for someone who was old enough at the time to still hold a grudge now, then by your logic our killer is a pensioner who fills his spare time between episodes of Homes Under The Hammer by carrying dead bodies halfway across Rutland in the middle of the night. Besides, why wait until now if they've been holding a grudge for fifty years? I'm not sure I buy it.'

'Me neither. And that's why we need to look further into it. Get a bit of context, if nothing else.'

'I get that, Dex. And I appreciate it. But we have to prioritise. We need to speak to Roger Clifton's staff and colleagues. And the council. And his family. We're far more likely to find motives there than we are reading history books. Know the victim, find the killer. That's my motto.'

'Totally agree,' Dexter said. 'Which is why I've arranged to visit Arthur Clifton Construction at midday today. The office'll be closed for a few days, but I got hold of his office manager and she's agreed to meet us. I also left a message with two councillors this morning and I'll ring the main council office as soon as it opens at nine.'

Caroline nodded her approval. 'Nicely done, Dex. Much appreciated.'

A couple of hours later, Caroline and Dexter arrived in Burley for their meeting with Roger Clifton's office manager, having driven the two miles from the office. When they arrived, a woman in her late forties was waiting for them at the gate. She wore a hi-vis jacket — something that struck Caroline as completely unnecessary if the yard was closed, but she supposed it was just habit. Grief did strange things to people.

'Sonya Smith?' Caroline called out the car window.

'Yeah, that's me,' Sonya said, almost inaudibly, as Caroline parked her car next to a portakabin. They got out of the car and followed Sonya inside, noticing two large men leaning against a storage unit in the main yard, watching their every move.

When they got inside, Sonya sat down behind her desk, waiting for Caroline to speak.

'Detective Inspector Caroline Hills. This is Detective

Sergeant Dexter Antoine. First of all, can I just say how sorry we are for your loss.'

Sonya nodded. 'Thank you. I know it sounds a bit weird, but we're not really sure what we *have* lost. No-one knows what happens now.'

'Who are those guys?' Dexter asked, gesturing through the window to the two men leaning against the storage unit in the yard.

'They work here. When we heard the news yesterday, I phoned round everyone to let them know. Said we'd be closed for a few days until we know what's going on. Word must've got round that I was meeting you here today, because they rocked up at the same time, wanting to know if they were going to get paid or have any work in the future.'

'A difficult situation, I can imagine,' Caroline said. No work meant no money. 'What's the setup of the company like? Does someone else automatically take over?'

Sonya raised her hands in a shrug of futility. 'Who knows? Roger ran everything on his own, pretty much. I did all the office stuff, but anything to do with the operation of the business was all down to him. I don't have a clue what's going on or who I can turn to. Those guys out there want to know when we're going to be open and working again. I don't know if we even can. What's the protocol? I've put a call in to the solicitor, but I've got no idea if he's ever going to ring me back. And with those two breathing down my neck and sending messages back and forth to the others, I feel like I want to scream.'

'We can ask them to leave, if you like,' Dexter said. 'If the business is closed, they don't need to be here.'

'To be honest, I've got bigger things to worry about right now. I just need the space to digest things, work out what's meant to happen with the business. Hopefully the solicitor can help me, because otherwise I don't know what's going to happen. I checked Companies House online, and Roger's the only director of the company. I don't know if that means it automatically passes to someone else, or who that person might even be. Or does it mean the company no longer exists? I don't know. This is what I need to find out.'

'Okay, let's calm down and take a breath,' Caroline said. 'The solicitor will be able to help you with all that. For now, it's best we focus on the questions we need to ask and the information we need to get to the bottom of what's happened. That way we can progress the case and hopefully draw a line under that side of things for you.' Sonya took a couple of deep breaths and nodded. 'So, what can you tell me about Roger? Do you know any reason why anyone would want him dead?'

A look crossed Sonya's face, almost as if it was the first time it had occurred to her that someone was actually responsible for this.

'No, I don't know,' she said. 'I mean, it's construction. There are always people for and against every project. But that's just how it goes. There are tens of thousands of construction projects going on around the country at any given time. People don't just go around murdering people because of them.'

'Have you had any particularly strong opposition to any projects recently?' Caroline asked. 'Does anything spring to mind as having been abnormal?'

Sonya thought for a moment before answering. 'No. Nothing. I mean, I can send you details of all our projects, if you like. You're more than welcome to look through and see if anything jumps out at you.'

'That'd be very useful,' Caroline replied, even though it was something she had intended to request anyway. 'Thank you. And what about family? What do you know about the situation there?'

Sonya thought for a moment, then shook her head. 'As far as I know, he's lived on his own since his marriage broke down. His wife lives in Empingham with their daughter. He's got a brother in Spain, I think, but he doesn't really talk about family stuff all that much.'

Bit strange, considering it was meant to be a family business, Caroline thought to herself. 'A brother?' she asked.

Sonya raised her hands in mock surrender. 'Don't ask me any more than that. Honestly, that's literally all I know. Just something he mentioned in passing once. I don't know any more than that.'

Caroline and Dexter shared a look. Both seemed to realise the same thing at the same time. If the family business had passed down from Arthur to Roger Clifton, might this mysterious missing brother have had an interest? In any case, it was a new connection — one they'd only discovered by speaking to Sonya Smith.

'You don't happen to remember the brother's name, I suppose?' Caroline asked.

Sonya screwed up her face and slowly shook her head. 'I don't, no. I've never met him and Roger never talked much about him. Sorry. I genuinely wish I could be more help.'

Caroline and Dexter stayed at the site for another forty minutes, trying to extract as much information from Sonya as they could. But it seemed information was a scarce resource. It appeared Roger Clifton had run the company almost single-handed, with Sonya handling invoices, payments, rotas and the like. She claimed never to have been involved with any of the company administration, and that anything more than mild bookkeeping was handled by Roger and his accountant.

'We'll need to look deeper into the financial affairs of the company,' Caroline said as they left the site and got back into the car. 'There's always a good chance money's at the root of this. It tends to be, more often than not.'

Dexter wanted to point out that EMSOU had dedicated financial analysis units which could look into precisely that sort of thing, but decided against it. He didn't know a huge amount about Caroline, but he did pride himself on being a good judge of character. And he'd judged that once Caroline made her mind up about something, there would be no consideration of turning round or going back.

He felt he got on with her, but he was aware this was probably more down to his own relaxed attitude and people skills than hers. He could see she wasn't a bad person; she just had a lot to learn if she was going to get on in a place like Rutland.

'A few of us are going for a couple of drinks after work if you want to join us,' he said.

'What, again?'

'Yeah. No harm in it. Nice chance to wind down after a long day.'

'Not tonight,' Caroline said, keeping her eyes on the road. 'Thanks for the offer, though,' she added a little while later, as if the thought had only just occurred to her.

Dexter smiled to himself. He could see he had work to do.

8

They arrived back at the station to find Sara Henshaw waiting for them with news.

'I've been doing the family liaison bit with Roger Clifton's wife,' she said. 'She's not keen to come in for an interview, so I said we'd look to send a couple of officers round. She specifically asked for non-uniformed officers and an unmarked car.' Caroline raised an eyebrow. Sara smiled. 'I know. I said we'd see what we could do. I tried to get her to talk, and she mentioned something interesting. Apparently Roger has a brother living in Spain. Arthur, his name is — after the grandfather. Just to confuse things. I've put a request in with the Spanish authorities to locate him and get hold of him.'

Caroline looked at Dexter and smiled. They could have come back to the office with the killer's name and photographic evidence of them doing it, and the ever-efficient Sara would've already had them arrested, charged and wallowing in HMP Whitemoor.

'Good work, Sara,' Caroline said, choosing not to burst her bubble. 'What about links with religion or the church? Anything on that front?'

'Not that she mentioned, no. But I can do a bit more digging on that front if you think it'd be useful.'

'I think it'd be handy to know, considering the circumstances. Sonya Smith, the office manager at Arthur Clifton Construction is going to send over a list of their recent jobs. There's a half-decent chance Roger could've pissed someone off that way, but Sonya said nothing sprang to mind. At least if we've got a list, we can look into it and cross-reference any names that crop up elsewhere.'

'I don't suppose we can discount the possibility that he wasn't specifically targeted, can we?' Sara asked.

Caroline swallowed before answering. 'Well, we can't discount anything at this stage. But everything points to a targeted attack, so it's probably best we channel most of our resources in that direction. It wouldn't be helpful to make other assumptions, I don't think.'

And there it was again: the ruthless efficiency of Sara Henshaw. It had, of course, been at the back of Caroline's mind that Roger Clifton's murder might not have been targeted at all, and that it might not be the last, but that wasn't a thought she wanted to entertain.

'Have we found anything on CCTV?' she asked, directing her attention to Aidan Chilcott.

'Nothing yet,' Aidan replied, his face almost a grimace. 'It'll take a while to go through everything. It's possible the killer could have got onto the water from anywhere on the perimeter and rowed over to the causeway, so there's a huge amount to check.'

'Difficult, though,' Sara said. 'That'd carry its own risks. The body was laid out pretty neatly on the rocks. That'd be almost impossible to do from a boat, especially without mooring it.'

Caroline snapped her fingers and pointed at Sara. 'Yes! And anyone who tried mooring their boat on those rocks would've scraped the bottom of the boat. There'd be paint transfer of some sort, without a shadow of a doubt. Let's get that checked out forensically.'

A phone rang, and Sara got up to answer it.

'Are we checking the boats or the rocks?' Dexter asked.

Caroline thought for a moment. 'The rocks. Anyone can hire out a boat, so I imagine ninety percent of them will have all sorts of scratches and scuffs. We'd be there forever. And we can't discount someone having brought their own boat along for the job. I think it's safe to say we'll find fewer scuff marks on the rocks at Normanton than we will on the bottom of hire boats, so let's go for that.'

'Won't the water have washed it all away, though? I can't imagine many paint flecks sticking around,' Aidan said.

'Quite possibly. But if we don't look, we won't find. And as things stand, we have no idea how our killer managed to reach the causeway, but if we can either rule a couple of things out or prioritise more likely scenarios, we'll get much closer. As far as I understand it, there are some "official" entrances to the water, some of which are covered with CCTV and ANPR, but there are a million ways to get there by foot. Of course, the fact our suspect was likely carrying a dead body does reduce the likelihood of that. Early signs are that Roger wasn't killed where he was found. There's no blood spatter, no sign of a local scuffle. So he's been brought to the site already dead. If you had an accomplice you could probably jump a wall, use a wheelbarrow, even carry a lightweight boat to the edge of the water. An accomplice makes things difficult in other areas, though. It means our killer is relying on someone else keeping quiet. That takes a huge amount of trust.'

'Unless two people wanted him dead,' Aidan said.

'Well, indeed.'

Sara Henshaw walked back towards them, looking a little sheepish and awkward after ending the incoming phone call.

'Okay. That was a message to say we've found a potential point of entry for our killer.'

Caroline's ears pricked up. 'What? Where?'

'There's an official service gate for Normanton Church at the junction of Wytchley Road and Normanton Park Road. It's usually locked and chained, but it's just been reported that the padlock appears to have been removed with bolt cutters.'

'Sorry, "just been reported"?' Caroline said, incensed. 'Did nobody think to check? We've spent god knows how long trying to come up with theories about how our killer got access to the causeway, and no-one thought to check the bloody front gate?'

The assembled officers shuffled uneasily, avoiding eye contact with Caroline.

'Right. Perfect. Thank you, Sara,' she said, rubbing her head. 'You and Aidan can follow that one up. Dex, with me. Let's go for a bit of light stress relief by spending an hour talking to a grieving wife.'

9

Caroline and Dexter drove out to Empingham, a village on the eastern side of Rutland Water — and home to Alice Clifton.

Dexter looked over at Caroline a couple of times as she drove, prompting her to ask him if something was on his mind.

'No, nothing,' he said. 'Just I've got a couple of interesting facts about Empingham and I was trying to work out if you were in an "Oooh that's interesting" mood or a "Piss off and leave me alone" mood.'

Caroline chuckled. 'Fire away, Dex. I'd love to hear them.'

'Alright. Well, first up, Empingham's protected from certain destruction only by a wall. To be more specific, a dam. It forms the eastern edge of Rutland Water. You can walk along it. If it wasn't there, the Empingham valley to the east would flood, along with the village.'

'Very good. Already knew it. What's the other one?'

'One of the battles of the Wars of the Roses took place there. The Battle of Empingham, believe it or not. Closest you'll get these days is some bloke getting an uppercut outside the White Horse.'

Caroline smiled. 'Where does it all come from, Dex? The trivia. The joy for learning. The boyish enthusiasm for just about everything.'

Dexter shrugged. 'I dunno. I just sort of enjoy it, you know? I think it's a rebellion thing.'

'How so?'

'Well, when I was a kid my parents really pushed me to do well at school. They wanted me to be a doctor. Thing is, the harder they pushed, the more I rebelled. So, I just about scraped through. Enough to make sure I'd be able to get a job and not totally screw my life up, I mean, but there was no way in hell anyone was going to let me study Medicine at Cambridge.'

'Wow. How'd they take that?'

'They switched their energies to my younger brother instead. He's training to become a gynaecologist. And yes, he's heard all the jokes.'

'There must be a deep love of learning in there somewhere, though. You certainly seem keen enough to me.'

'Oh yeah, definitely. I just like doing it on my own terms, you know? I think joining the police was a bit of a rebellion, too.'

'What, you didn't actually want to do it?'

Dexter shook his head. 'Not really. But I didn't know

what I wanted to do, and I figured this'd piss my parents off the most.'

Caroline laughed. 'Well, it was a good move on all counts. You're not too bad at it, you know.'

They arrived at the address in Empingham, greeted by an elaborate set of cast-iron gates. The house that stood at the end of the driveway beyond was impressive, to say the least. It was clear Roger Clifton had earned some money in his time, especially if he was happy to live elsewhere and leave this place to his wife.

'Blimey. Who'd have thought it?' Dexter said. 'You've got wankers putting signs saying "Elm Cottage" and "The Willows" on their two-bed semi, then you run into a mansion like this — house number 27. Crazy.'

Before Caroline could get out of the car, the gates clicked and whirred open, allowing them to coast up the long gravel driveway towards the front of the house. As they reached it, the front door opened and a woman stepped out.

She was clearly younger than Roger had been — forty, tops. Her body language made it seem more like she was welcoming an old friend, as opposed to the police officers investigating her husband's death.

'Hi, Alice Clifton. Pleasure to meet you. Come on in,' she said, her voice like velvet.

The hallway was more akin to the lobby of a posh hotel than someone's actual house, and there was a clear rivalry between marble and gold leaf for the title of Most Overused Material. Alice led Caroline and Dexter through to a large kitchen diner, seating them at a long, ornate counter —

marble, naturally. It occurred to Caroline that marble wasn't the ideal choice of stone in a kitchen and wondered what Alice Clifton did about the inevitable staining, but quickly realised she'd probably just shell out a few grand on a new one.

Once the formalities were cleared, Caroline decided to get down to some more detailed questioning.

'Can you describe your relationship with your husband for me?' she asked, before taking a sip of the hot black coffee Alice had placed in front of her.

She looked at Caroline for a moment before speaking. 'That's an odd way of putting it. Who've you been talking to? Oh, I guess it doesn't matter. Everyone's relationship is different, isn't it? Roger and I weren't the *conventional* couple, if that's what you mean. I think "estranged" is probably the word you'd use.'

'Can you elaborate please?'

'Well, Roger hadn't lived here for a while. He had other properties and had been living between those. We were still married, officially, but I think we both knew deep down that was only the case on paper. If you catch my drift.'

'I think so. Had you spoken about divorce at all?'

Alice shook her head and made a face that looked as if Caroline had just asked her if she'd ever considered fellating a horse. 'Absolutely not. That's not the sort of thing we *do*.'

'I see. But did you still get on?'

'We didn't hate each other, if that's what you mean. I was probably the only one who didn't despise him.'

'Go on,' Caroline said, leaning in.

'Roger didn't exactly make friends easily. He found

enemies came much more naturally. But I guess that's the nature of business and local politics, isn't it?'

'I'd hope not, but maybe so.'

'Do you have any examples?' Dexter asked.

'Oh, he used to get plenty of angry and threatening emails. Usually over planning applications of one sort or another. If he wasn't connected with the development or construction in a business sense, he almost certainly would be in a political sense. People get angry about those sorts of things round here. They don't like change.'

'These emails,' Dexter said, trying to get the conversation back on track. 'Where might we be able to find them?'

'Well, you'd have to check his work laptop. He didn't really use it much, though. His office manager used to deal with most of that stuff. Sonya, her name is. Sometimes he'd get them on his personal account too, but not that often.'

'And how did this affect family life?' Caroline asked. 'You have a daughter, don't you?'

'Yes, Hannah,' Alice said, smiling.

'And she's how old?'

'Nineteen.'

Caroline did a quick bit of mental maths. If Alice was around forty, she must have had Hannah quite young. It also meant Roger Clifton was around forty when he fathered a child with a woman not long out of school herself. 'Does she live with you?' Caroline asked.

'She does, but she's not in at the moment. She's popped out to see some friends. You know how they are at that age.'

Caroline smiled and nodded. She did. She also knew

there was no way a nineteen-year-old girl would leave her mobile phone on the kitchen work surface, and that it was very unlikely her mother would own the latest iPhone with a pink sparkly protective case that said *Glamour Bitch*.

'I don't suppose you happen to be religious, do you?' Caroline asked.

'Why do you ask?'

'I just wondered. You seemed to imply that divorce wasn't an option,' she said, thinking on her feet.

'Well that has nothing to do with religion. I'm a Methodist.'

Caroline tried not to show too much of a reaction to this news. 'Oh? And Roger too, presumably?'

Alice laughed. 'No. Not Roger. Not by a long shot. He used to call it a load of old hogwash. I go to church every Sunday, but I think the only times Roger set foot in a church were on our wedding day and when Hannah got baptised. He wouldn't even come to events there with me. The couple of times he did, he always rubbed people up the wrong way.'

Caroline nodded as she pretended to jot down a few things in her notebook. In fact, there were only two words, which she left in full view of Dexter.

Told you.

'Well, this is all very helpful, Mrs Clifton. Thank you. Would you mind if I used the bathroom, please?'

'No, of course,' Alice said, gesturing in the general direction of the hall.

'Thanks. Still getting used to the Indian takeaways around here. Bit different to London.'

She smiled inwardly to herself as she thought of Dexter being left in the kitchen with Alice Clifton on the back of that little comment. At least it'd give her a good few minutes to do what she'd really come here for.

10

The upstairs of Alice Clifton's house was still palatial, but less ornate and tacky than much of the downstairs had been. Caroline wondered to herself whether downstairs had been styled for other people to see, whereas the upstairs had been purely for Alice and her daughter.

She wandered into the main bathroom and splashed some water on her face. She supposed she should at least make a show of having actually been in the bathroom.

Caroline prided herself on having a good eye and ear for detail. It was something that had been pointed out to her early on in her career, and was what had made her first consider a route to CID. It was that eagle eye which had spotted the mobile phone in the kitchen downstairs, and her keen ear that made her sure she'd heard someone shuffling around as she came up the stairs.

She walked back across the landing, taking slow steps, and saw a slight shadow moving in the gap underneath one of the bedroom doors. She moved towards it and whispered.

'Hannah?'

There was a brief moment before the door opened and Caroline came face to face with a beautiful young woman she assumed to be Hannah Clifton. 'Can I come in?' Caroline mouthed, gesturing towards the room. The girl nodded and stepped to the side, allowing Caroline to enter before closing the door quietly behind them.

'I'm guessing you're from the police,' Hannah said, her eyes red. 'You've got that look about you.'

'I'm not quite sure how to take that, so I'll just say thanks. I'm sorry about your father,' she said, noticing that Hannah had clearly been crying. It seemed odd that her mother appeared to have no such remorse about her husband's death.

'Thank you. He was an amazing man.'

'Can you tell me a little bit about him?'

'I don't really know what to say, to be honest. He was… strong. He didn't take no for an answer. Never. He always knew what he wanted and he made damn sure he got it. I hope I can take after him.'

Caroline didn't particularly fancy the idea of her children turning out like either Roger or Alice, but having spent some time with the latter she knew which she'd choose if push came to shove.

'Your mum said you weren't home.'

Hannah made a noise like the brakes on a bus. 'She's full of shit. She wanted me out of the way when you guys came over, because she thought I might say "the wrong thing".'

'I don't think there is a wrong thing or a right thing to say. The only thing we want is the truth.'

Hannah cocked her head and waved a finger. 'I know, right? That's what I said to her, but she wasn't having it. She likes to be seen as this perfect little housewife, the dedicated churchgoer who can't do any wrong. It's all bullshit.'

'How so?'

Hannah dropped onto the bed in a seated position, bouncing a couple of times as the mattress fought back. 'She's been hanging out with this rugby guy a lot lately. He used to be a pro, apparently. Like, back in the seventeenth century or something. Mum says they're just friends, but she doesn't know a thing about rugby. They're clearly banging.'

Caroline raised an eyebrow. 'And what makes you say that?'

'I know these things. You should see the way they look at each other. It's gross. Shame, too. I'd *totally* go there.'

'What, with the rugby guy?'

'Patrick,' Hannah said, as if she'd already told Caroline his name and she was being rude by not using it. 'And yeah, totally. For an old guy he's pretty hot. He's, like, all muscles and stuff. Super yum.'

Caroline nodded slowly, the cogs turning in her brain as she tried to figure out the odd family dynamic. 'And when you say old…'

'Oh, he's like mid-forties, probably? Younger than Dad, but still proper old. Your sort of age. Not, like, grandad age but still plenty of juice left in the tank.'

'I see. You like older men, do you?'

'Wouldn't be the first time. They tend to be more… appreciative.'

'Do you have a photo of Patrick?' Caroline asked, keen to keep the conversation clean and professional.

'Well, yeah. Just Google the guy.' Hannah stood up and walked over to her desk, before tapping a couple of keys on her laptop to wake it up. She logged in, pulled up a browser tab and typed *Patrick Walsh* into Google Images. 'There you go. Fit or what?'

Caroline had to admit he wasn't bad at all, but refrained from saying so. She took her mobile phone from her pocket and snapped a couple of pictures of the screen.

'Urgh. Old people are so *dumb*. You don't need to do that. Just Google him on your phone and download the images.'

'Well it's done now,' Caroline replied, smiling. As she went to put her phone back in her pocket, it began to vibrate. Sara Henshaw's name was on the screen. 'One sec,' she mouthed to Hannah, stepping out of the room. 'Sara?'

'Thought you might like to know, one of the councillors called me back. Barbara Tallis, her name is. She's free tomorrow morning and happy to meet for a chat.'

Caroline smiled. She had a feeling that could be very useful indeed.

11

'Who'd he play for?' Caroline asked as they walked into town the next morning to meet Councillor Barbara Tallis.

'Leicester Tigers, apparently,' Dexter replied, reading off his phone. 'Local lad, played his whole career there. Even got a few games for Ireland.'

'Ooh, properly local then.'

'His parents are Irish. You know what it's like with international sport. If you order a takeaway once a week they let you play for China.'

'Is he married?'

'Dunno,' Dexter said, grimacing at his phone. 'Can't see any mention of a wife here, but I'll keep looking.'

Before long, the looming spire of the Church of All Saints was behind them and the marketplace opened in front.

The Lord Nelson was a traditional characterful pub tucked away in the corner of the marketplace, with the original building dating back to the 1500s. They ordered two coffees at the bar, then made their way through the labyrinthine corridors and up the stairs.

'Christ, this place is like a maze,' Caroline said, trying not to spill her coffee.

'Don't tell me you've never been here before,' Dexter replied, already knowing what the answer would be.

'I'm not really a pub person.'

'It's not just a pub. It's the heart of the community. Then again, I don't suppose that appeals either, does it?' he said, checking one of the upstairs lounge rooms and finding it empty.

'Why do you say that?'

'Because you're not community-minded and you don't have a heart. Ah! You must be Councillor Tallis. DS Antoine. Lovely to meet you.'

Caroline knew he'd timed his barb perfectly and would spend the rest of the meeting with a smug grin on his face, knowing all she wanted to do was put him right.

Even if the Lord Nelson had been heaving with people, Barbara Tallis would have been the clear favourite in a Spot The Councillor competition. And from the way she spoke, it seemed she had a number of years' of experience in local politics under her belt.

'Terrible news about Roger,' she said, getting to the point. 'The way he died, I mean.'

'Were you close?' Caroline asked.

'I'm not entirely sure anyone was ever close to Roger. He was a… tricky character, let's say.'

'Go on.'

'Look, local politics is always swimming with rumours

and people making assumptions, but I guess that's the nature of the game. There were a few people — and I'm naming no names — who got the impression that Roger only came onto the council when it suited him, rather than because he wanted to do something for the local community.'

'With the greatest of respect,' Caroline said, 'you may well have to name names. This is a murder investigation.'

Dexter tried to settle the uneasy atmosphere. 'How did he keep getting voted back onto the council if he was that unpopular?'

'Oh, good Lord, that's not difficult. We have enough trouble trying to get people to stand as it is. Most wards and council seats are won unopposed, without us even getting so far as holding a vote. On the odd occasions people actually did stand against Roger, he always had just enough friends to be able to sneak back in. Anyone can get on the council by putting their name down, essentially. We've got vacancies at the moment, if either of you are interested.'

'I live in Leicester, unfortunately,' Dexter said, trying to remain diplomatic.

'And I follow Groucho Marx's philosophy of not joining any club that'd have me as a member,' Caroline added, her attempt at humour not quite hitting its mark.

'Yes, well, it's more of a civic responsibility than a "club", and I must say that sort of attitude is what breeds low levels of engagement in the first place.'

'Can you give me any examples of times when Roger's time on the council might have been linked with vested interests?' Dexter asked, trying to return to matters of business once again.

'Oh, I could give you a list as long as my arm. But it was mostly to do with planning. Roger was in construction, see? He had a lot of connections in that industry, and there was always talk of him greasing the wheels to push things through. There are measures in place to make sure that doesn't happen, of course. Any new councillor has to declare interests, and usually those will stop them from sitting on specific committees. Roger never sat on the planning committee, for example, but he still had great influence. Some of the other councillors had particular projects or ideas they wanted to put through other committees, and Roger would — rumour has it — take on their causes in exchange for a... let's say slightly more laissez-faire attitude to the occasional planning application.'

'Vote swapping?'

'Influence swapping, perhaps. He never directly approached me with anything like that, but then again he knew I wouldn't stand for it. I'm on the council for the right reasons, I can tell you that. Besides which, it wasn't just a case of exchanging a few votes.'

'Oh?' Caroline asked, her interest piqued.

'I never saw anything. Not directly. Again, this is just rumour and hearsay, and there's plenty of that on local councils. But there were occasional mentions of brown envelopes being passed beneath tables.'

'You mean Roger Clifton bribed other councillors to pass planning applications?'

'I wouldn't want to cast aspersions or make accusations.

All I can tell you is what I've been told. And no, those people didn't accept the money. They wouldn't have told me if they had, but I think we can safely assume there must have been others who did accept it and who've stayed quiet. He had his friends on the council, there was no doubt about that, but for the most part he wasn't particularly well-liked by the members and was always seen as a bit of a wide-boy.'

'Is that normal around here?' Caroline asked.

'Sorry, what do you mean?'

'I mean, it's a rural area. Small. Everyone knows each other. I came from London, and the corruption on the councils there was bad enough. I imagine in a place like this there's a fair bit of behind-the-scenes discussion and decisions reached before meetings even take place, no?'

Barbara Tallis didn't need to say a word. Her face clearly conveyed the answer.

'Well that went well,' Dexter said as they got back into Caroline's car a short while later.

'I don't know what it is with people round here,' Caroline said, sighing as she put on her seatbelt. 'She's not the first person to get the hump with me recently. I mean, I know rural communities are backward, but I didn't think they still did the whole "you're not local" thing. Sometimes I reckon I'd feel more welcome in North Korea.'

'I don't think it's anything to do with not being local. You live in Oakham. Can't get much more local than that.'

'Not originally, though. I'm from London. I'm an

outsider. Places like this aren't ever going to accept people like me.'

Dexter turned in his seat. 'Okay. First of all, I'm not local either and I've never had any issues.'

'You're from Leicester, Dex. That's local enough.'

'Yeah, and have you seen the colour of my skin? If people round here were that "anti-local", they'd have lynched me by now. Besides which, there's no such thing as local. Hardly anyone in Rutland is "local". It's a proper melting pot of accents and backgrounds. People move here from all over the place. Anyone "local" tends to have moved out years ago for silly little things like, you know, actual jobs.'

'Leaving only the retired folk to come here and treat it as God's waiting room, complete with their disdain for anyone else wanting to make the same move they did, you mean?'

Dexter turned away and looked out his window. 'I've seen no evidence of that, and I've been working here a lot longer than you.'

'All I can say is what I see.'

'Yeah, exactly. Me too.'

'What does that mean?'

'Nothing.'

'Go on. Tell me,' Caroline said.

'It's nothing to do with the people round here. They're fine. It's just… It's a different way of life. It's friendlier.'

'I'm friendly. I can do friendly.'

'By London standards? Yeah, maybe. But friendly by London standards is not deliberately walking into people in the street, or gently closing the door on a stranger instead of slamming it in their face.'

'Okay, now we're in the realms of silliness, Dex.'

'We're not. We're really not. I'm just being honest. I know these people. I know the area. And you're just too… Londony. I know you don't do it on purpose, and it's not even necessarily a bad thing. It just doesn't work round here. You come across as cold and standoffish. I know you're not. I know it's just where you've come from. But maybe it means you need to adapt a little for the area. You keep pointing out to everyone how different things are round here, and making sweeping assumptions about the way things are and the way they must be because it's "that sort of place". It sounds rude. Rutland's a really bloody friendly place, if you actually allow yourself to integrate.'

'Right,' Caroline said, turning the car into the car park of the police station. 'Well, that's certainly put me in my place.'

Dexter let out a huge sigh. 'I wasn't trying to put you in your place. I was trying to make you see that all this is just a clash of cultures. You can't ask the entire county to change for you, but if you're aware of how you come across to people, maybe you can tweak things and enjoy your time here a lot more. Look, a few of us are going for drinks after work again tonight. Why don't you join us? I know it's not your usual scene, but it might do you good. Call it integrating, if you like.'

Caroline had been biting her lip for a while, and was in no mood to consider drinks and jollities. 'I'm fine, thanks,' she said. 'Maybe another time.'

Caroline awoke the next morning with a now-familiar roiling sensation in the pit of her stomach. The nausea came and went and could largely be managed, but sometimes the queasiness made its intentions quite clear. She opened the door of the ensuite bathroom, fell to her knees and vomited into the toilet. It had been a couple of weeks since she'd felt this bad, but she'd been expecting it to return. She could almost set her clock by it — the constant reminder that things didn't always go as planned.

Ten minutes later, once the spell had passed, she got herself washed and dressed and made her way downstairs. Mark was waiting in the kitchen for her.

'Boys, why don't you nip through to the playroom for a bit? You can even watch some telly if you like. Special treat.'

Caroline knew immediately that Mark wanted to have words with her. He'd never broken the no-TV-before-school rule before. She watched as Archie and Josh disappeared from the kitchen and headed down the hallway and into the playroom. It had been listed as the dining room on the floor plan when they'd looked at the house, but the large kitchen extension with space for its own ten-seater dining table meant the other room was always destined to be filled with toys and junk.

'What's wrong?' she asked, looking at Mark.

'Are you alright? I mean… is everything okay?'

'Of course it is,' she replied. 'Why wouldn't it be?'

'I heard you being sick.'

'Oh, that. I don't know what that was. Probably something I ate yesterday. It was weird, but it's passed now. I'll keep an eye on it, but really, I wouldn't worry.'

'Caroline, it's not the first time. I've heard you being sick a few times recently. In the mornings.'

She didn't want to lie to Mark by telling him he was mistaken. There was a difference between not telling someone something and actively lying to them. 'It's fine. Probably just stress or a tummy bug or something.'

'It's been happening a lot.'

'Yeah, well, I've been stressed a lot. And eating shit at work. I'll try and get some time booked off and cut down on the takeaways. I'll be fine.'

'Are you pregnant?'

'What?'

'You heard me. It's all adding up now. The morning sickness. Not wanting to drink the wine. I saw your face when you sniffed it the other night. It was like you were sniffing vinegar. The wine was fine. It was lovely, in fact.'

Caroline blinked and tried to push down the feelings that were now welling up from deep inside her. 'Sorry, you think I'm pregnant because I didn't like the same wine as you?'

'Come on, Caroline. We haven't exactly been careful, have we? It's entirely possible, to say the least. Have you done a test?'

'No. I haven't. Because I don't need to do a test, Mark. I'm not pregnant. I know I'm not pregnant. Is that good enough for you?'

'Well, no. How can you possibly know without a test?'

'Because I'm a woman, Mark. Women know their bodies.'

'What, and you know it's perfectly normal to wake up and empty your guts down the toilet on a regular basis?'

'If I'm stressed, anxious or not eating properly, yes. That's perfectly normal.'

'Or pregnant.'

'I'm not pregnant, Mark.'

'Do a test then. If you're that sure, do a test.'

Caroline gritted her teeth. 'Do you realise how insulting that is? A woman knows her body, Mark. I'm not pregnant. If you want to do a test, you can shove it up your arse.'

'Yeah, I don't think that's quite how they work,' he called out to the back of her head as she headed back up the stairs. 'Jesus fucking Christ.'

13

One of Mark's biggest virtues was that he knew when to give up. Caroline was thankful that he was usually pretty good at respecting her need for space, especially when he never seemed to need any himself.

Shortly after the exchange with Mark, Dexter phoned her. He'd got to work early again, and had taken a message from the minister at Empingham Methodist Church, returning Caroline's call and saying he'd be delighted to meet her. Dexter had barely disguised the disapproving tone in his voice as he'd relayed this to her, but that didn't bother Caroline. There were too many coincidences to ignore, and she felt sure there must be a religious connection to the death of Roger Clifton — particularly since discovering his vocal atheism and his wife's connection to the church.

Dexter told her he'd walk out to the bypass so they could drive over together. When Caroline arrived, she saw her colleague had bought her a large takeaway coffee.

'You didn't need to do that, Dex.'

'I know. It kept my hands warm while I was walking. And I know how grumpy you can be in the mornings. Don't want you upsetting any more locals, do we?'

The boyish grin on Dexter's face made it impossible for Caroline to be angry at him.

'Thank you,' she said, pulling back out onto the road.

'So. The reverend. Is there a new line I've missed?'

'Nope, same one, still valid. Perhaps even more so, after the chat with Alice and Hannah Clifton.'

'What, an ex-rugby star turns psychopathic killer and fancies bumping off a local businessman because he's not keen on going to church jumble sales?'

'Local businessman and his lover's husband,' Caroline added. 'His churchgoing, religious lover.'

'Reading between the lines, I doubt if he was too bothered about that. They were separated. "Estranged" was the word, wasn't it? And in any case, that might give Roger Clifton a reason to want to bump off Patrick Walsh, but probably not the other way round.'

'Unless Alice Clifton thought she might be in line to inherit the family business. That'd give them a nice little payout, wouldn't it? Perfect opportunity to set up a new life on their own.'

Dexter grimaced. 'I don't see it. Look at the size of the gaff she's got already. And he's an ex-rugby international, so he's not exactly short of a few bob either. I think murdering the ex and laying him out in the middle of Rutland Water for all to see would probably be a risk too far, especially when it ends up pointing so deliberately towards them. It's almost *too* convenient.'

'I'll bear it in mind.'

They arrived in Empingham a few minutes later, having skirted the North Shore along the A606, before turning into the village and pulling up outside the church.

'You'd think he might've suggested a coffee shop or something,' Caroline said.

'What, in Empingham?'

Caroline sighed. 'Fair point. Shall we?'

As soon as they stepped inside the church, they were greeted by a genial-looking man who introduced himself as the Reverend Peter Tottman.

'Thanks for getting back to me so quickly,' Caroline said. 'I appreciate you must be very busy.' In finding the Reverend's contact number, she'd discovered he was not only the minister at Empingham, but also Oakham and Uppingham Methodist Churches.

'I'm only here to help get a few things in order for the fete on Saturday, but I'm more than happy to help,' the reverend said, smiling.

'I realise this might be a bit uncomfortable or unconventional, but we're currently investigating the murder of a man called Roger Clifton. Does the name ring any bells?'

The look on Peter Tottman's face told Caroline it did. 'Alice's ex-husband. Yes, I heard the news. Terrible.'

'Well, husband,' Caroline said. 'They were still married.'

'I see. And how can I help?'

'We understand Roger wasn't exactly a keen churchgoer. Is that right?'

Peter Tottman smiled again. 'I think we can safely say he didn't share the same faith as his wife.'

'And did that cause any problems among the congregation?'

'Oh no,' the Reverend said, with the slightest of laughs. 'Not in the slightest. Don't worry, we're not under the impression that everyone either is or should be a practising Christian.'

'And do you know of anyone who might've had a falling out of some sort with Roger?'

'Not through the church, no. I understand he was in business. Construction. And he was active on the local council, of course. That's a surefire way to pick up an odd sort of fan club, I'm sure. But I'm not aware of him falling out with anyone within the local church community. These are good people. Christians.'

'What can you tell me about Alice Clifton? Is she a good person? A devout Christian?'

'I've known Alice through the church for some time. And yes, she strikes me as a good person.'

'And what about her relationship status? What's your understanding of that?'

'Sorry, I'm not quite sure what it is you're insinuating.'

'Are you aware of any — how can I put it — extra-marital exploits on Alice's part?'

'I think that's a question you'd need to put to her, Detective Inspector. I'm not really in the habit of idle gossiping, particularly not about members of my congregation.'

Dexter shuffled awkwardly.

'I don't think now's the time to batten down the hatches,' Caroline said. 'This is a murder investigation.'

'I understand that perfectly well.'

'Then you can tell me what you know about Alice Clifton and Patrick Walsh, can't you?'

Peter Tottman looked at her for a few moments before speaking. 'I'm sorry,' he said. 'I'm going to have to ask you to leave.'

14

'Tell me that didn't strike you as suspicious,' Caroline said, as they got into the car and headed back to Oakham.

'It wasn't an ideal outcome,' Dexter said, trying to remain diplomatic as always.

'You know, I had half a mind to arrest him. I was *this* close. Then he'd have no choice but to talk. The Police and Criminal Evidence Act doesn't protect church ministers from spreading social gossip, so far as I understand it.'

'You wanted to arrest a minister because he didn't want to get into rumours and hearsay over one of his parishioners?'

'They aren't rumours and hearsay. Alice Clifton's own daughter told us that much. You saw his face when I mentioned Patrick Walsh's name. There's something very odd going on there.'

'Or maybe it just wasn't the most sensitive line of questioning. Emotions are running high. Religious communities can be quite tight-knit. Perhaps a gentler approach might have worked better.'

Caroline sighed. 'It's a murder investigation, Dex. There's nothing gentle about it.'

Caroline had been looking forward to assembling the team for a briefing and update, but she'd barely been in the office thirty seconds when there was a knock at the door.

With such a small police force, it wasn't uncommon to see Chief Superintendent Derek Arnold roaming the corridors, but an unannounced visit was never usually good news.

'Caroline, do you have a moment?' he asked, gesturing for her to follow him. She said nothing, but headed after him in the direction of his office.

Unlike most larger police forces, who tended to have a number of superior officers at each level, Rutland Police's set-up was far more basic — 'streamlined', as the police press office liked to call it. Due to Rutland's size, the Chief Superintendent was also the de facto Assistant and Deputy Chief Constable. Although his pay grade didn't back that up, it was almost certain he'd be next in line to take the role of Chief Constable, as and when Jane Condry decided she'd had enough and wanted to vacate the top job.

Derek Arnold's office was no plusher than the other rooms in the oversized scout hut Rutland Police called home, but being called in to see a superior officer always gave their space an additional aura.

'I just wanted to call you in to let you know I've received a complaint,' Arnold said, getting straight to the point.

'A complaint?'

'Yes. From the Reverend Peter Tottman. I understand you went to see him this morning.'

'We did, yes. In connection with Operation Forelock. We have reason to believe there might be a religious connection.'

'I'm sure it's a distinct possibility. But that isn't the issue here. The complaint was with regards to your conduct and manner of questioning. The Reverend felt you'd been rude, disrespectful and brash.'

Caroline swallowed hard. 'I'm not sure I'd use any of those words to describe it, if I'm honest. I thought I was direct, polite and fair.'

'He disagrees. In a place like Rutland, forging and maintaining strong links with the local community is vital. It's a small place, Caroline. We can't afford to go pissing people off.'

'I understand that. But, with respect, this is a murder investigation. Hard questions need to be asked. I've got to say, I really didn't expect him to immediately jump on the phone to you to complain about me asking questions. Are you friends?'

'What's that supposed to mean?'

Caroline decided to try a different angle. 'Is this an official verbal warning?'

'Not this time, no.'

'So it wasn't an official complaint done through the official routes? Just a quick word in your ear?'

Arnold leaned forward on his desk, his arms crossed.

'Listen here. I don't know what you're trying to get at, but you need to stop it. I don't know how you did things in the Met, and to be frank I really don't care. You're not in London now. This isn't the Met. You're in Rutland. We treat people like human beings here. If you want people to help you and provide you with information, you need to show them respect. Trying to bully and frighten people isn't going to work, let me tell you that.'

'I'm not trying to bully or frighten anyone,' Caroline said, a nagging voice at the back of her head reminding her that Derek Arnold wasn't the first person this week to pull her up on her London-centric attitude. 'I'm just trying to get to bottom of what happened to Roger Clifton and make sure we do justice for him and his family. It's what every victim deserves.'

'I completely agree. We're fighting the same corner here, Caroline. But you're not going the right way about it. By rights, this is the sort of case we shouldn't even be handling. This should've gone to EMSOU. Do you have any idea what sort of shit I'm having to put up with from them? They're breathing down my neck like you wouldn't believe. Don't go giving me or them any reason to pull you off the case and hand it over, Caroline. Do you hear?'

She swallowed hard again. 'Yes, sir. I get it. Don't worry.'

As she left Derek Arnold's office, Caroline bumped into Dexter as he left the toilet.

'Alright?' he said.

'Yeah. Wonderful.'

Caroline looked at him. The awkward expression on her colleague's face told her all she needed to know. 'You heard all that, didn't you?'

Dexter shrugged. 'Thin walls in here. Whose bright idea was it to have the chief's office backing onto the men's bogs?'

'You didn't need the loo, did you?'

He shrugged again. 'Always good to keep regular. Don't be too downhearted, yeah? He's getting pressure from above him, and from the boys from EMSOU. And you know what people can be like. They'll complain about anything. He's only doing his job in passing it on.'

'You do know that was a private meeting, don't you? Confidential.'

'Hey, I didn't decide to build a police station out of cardboard. I can't help it if the sound leaks through, can I? I just wanted you to know I'm behind you. I support you.'

'Dex, I don't need support. I need you to get on with your job. We've got a killer to find. I don't need any more of this bullshit. Just focus on what you're meant to do, alright?'

15

Caroline made her way back to the incident room, Dexter trailing behind.

'Guv, we've had some preliminary post-mortem results on Roger Clifton,' Aidan Chilcott said, almost as soon as she'd entered the office.

'I hope it's good news, Aidan,' Caroline replied. 'I'm not in the mood for another spanner in the works right now.'

Aidan looked at her for a moment. 'Can post-mortem results ever be good news?' he asked.

'Depends whose post-mortem it is. What have you got for me?'

'No water in the lungs. Therefore, Roger Clifton didn't drown. The ligature marks round the neck are suspected to have been caused by nylon rope. Blunt force trauma to the head, potentially some form of metal or non-fibrous material. They haven't been able to pick up any wood splinters or rust or anything, so whatever it was, it was likely new. About an inch and a half in diameter, potentially rounded. I pushed for something a bit more specific and she said her best guess would be a crowbar or a lug wrench. Sort of thing most people would have in their car, anyway.'

'We're going with the car theory, then?'

'It's looking likely. Especially as the entry gate was broken. I can't see any reason why someone would go to the effort of doing that, then walk the rest of the way.'

'Okay. Even so, we're looking for someone with a certain amount of strength. The body will've had to have been lifted, even if someone did get the car all the way up to the church. They had to get it from the boot of the car, over the edge and onto the rocks. Let's face it — we're probably looking at a man, and a pretty strong one at that. Resourceful, too. Came equipped with bolt cutters for the gate. Had a crowbar or a — what was it?'

'Lug wrench.'

'One of those, yeah. He obviously knew what he was doing. Maybe we're looking for a mechanic of some sort. A builder? We know Arthur was heavily connected with the trades. It's entirely possible he's pissed off a builder at some time or another.'

'Would need to be more than pissing them off to result in premeditated murder, surely?'

'Maybe not a man of God after all,' Dexter said, unable to help himself.

'The killer went to a lot of effort to take a dead body there under cover of darkness and lay it out on the rocks in that specific place. I don't think we can overlook that.'

'No, but we shouldn't be using it as our pivot point, either. It's not the be-all-and-end-all, especially when there's far more compelling evidence like the tampering with the gate, big clues as to the murder weapon, knowledge that the killer had to actually bring the body to the dump site.'

'All things which heavily suggest the killer was very keen — almost desperate — to make sure the church *was* the dump site, Dex.'

'So why there? It hasn't been a church for fifty years. It's hardly a religious building anymore. There are dozens of churches in Rutland the killer could've chosen. I can't think of a single one that's harder to reach than Normanton. If it was about religion, he'd have picked another church — an *actual* church.'

'No. He specifically needed it to be this one.'

'Why?'

'I don't know. That's what we need to find out.'

'Then perhaps we should concentrate on what we do know.'

Caroline looked at Dexter, well aware that Sara Henshaw and Aidan Chilcott were shuffling awkwardly. 'Detective Sergeant Antoine, can I talk to you outside for a moment please?'

Without waiting for an answer, she walked out of the incident room and took a few steps further down the corridor. Dexter followed behind.

'Can you remind me who's in charge of this investigation, Detective Sergeant Antoine?'

'You are.'

'Correct. And before you say it, yes, I am aware we're a team and that we all need to pull our weight and offer suggestions. I know you don't think there's a religious connection with Roger Clifton's death. You've made that perfectly clear. But the location of the dump site is clearly a huge part of this, and all avenues will be investigated. And whilst I appreciate your enthusiasm in continually trying to hammer that home to me, I do not appreciate you doing so in front of the rest of the team. You're a good copper, Dex, but you need to wind your neck in, alright? I do not need you undermining me in my incident room. Do you understand?'

Dexter nodded, his teeth gritted hard. This time, he wasn't going to follow his boss back into the incident room; he was going to get a strong coffee.

16

The rest of the day passed in a blur of admin and collating everything that was known so far with regards to Operation Forelock. Caroline didn't mind, though. She was happy to be locked away on her own, unable to get pissed off or piss anyone else off.

It seemed to be a common thread recently that people got pissed off when she was around. It wasn't something that had ever bothered her too much. She just assumed that was how people were round here. But a few things Dexter had said recently had started to play on her mind. It wasn't normal for her. She didn't like being irritable. She wasn't interested in being a social animal, but at the same time she didn't want to fall out with anyone unnecessarily — especially not her colleagues or local people she might need to rely on in the future.

Towards the end of the day, she fired Mark a quick text then stepped out of her office and into the main incident room.

'Dex, have you got a sec?' she said, beckoning him towards her, trying hard to make sure her tone of voice implied he wasn't in for another bollocking. She closed the door to give them some privacy in her office. 'I just wanted to say sorry for the way I acted earlier. I didn't mean to be so harsh. It's great that you're keen, and I really value your work and your… your acquaintanceship.'

'My acquaintanceship?'

'Look, I wondered if you and the others were planning on having a drink after work again tonight.'

Dexter's eyebrows flicked upwards. 'Well, yeah. We kind of go most nights, to be honest. There's always at least a couple of us there. I only ever have a half, though, because I'm driving.'

'Yeah, I'm not trying to set up a drink-drive sting, Dex. I'm asking if I can come along and join you.'

'Tonight?'

'I mean, it doesn't have to be tonight. It can be any night. But I'm free tonight if that works.' On the plus side, it meant she wouldn't have to go home and face Mark for an extra couple of hours. She could do with keeping her mind off the argument they'd had earlier.

'Tonight works,' Dexter said.

Caroline smiled. 'Good. Looking forward to it. Thanks.'

An hour or so later, she was sitting at a table in the Wheatsheaf. She'd walked and driven past the pub hundreds of times, but had never set foot in it. It was a traditional town boozer — a selection of ales on handpumps, cider served from the cellar and signs advertising homemade pub food. She leaned over the bar to see which white wines were in the fridge — the thought of red still made her stomach turn — and was eyeing up the Pinot Grigio when Dexter whispered in her ear.

'If you're trying to ingratiate yourself with the locals, try a drop of that,' he said, pointing to one of the real ale pumps. Tiger, from Everard's Brewery.

'That's from Leicester,' she said.

'Yeah. When I said locals, I meant me.'

'You're a dick, Dex. I'll have a pint.'

'Blimey, in at the deep end. Don't you want to try a bit first?'

'What, and if I hate it you'll not be offended in the slightest?'

'No, I'd never speak to you again.'

'Tempting as that is, I need the alcohol. Pint please.'

As she'd fully intended, one pint became two, then three. Partway through her fourth, Sara and Aidan had made their excuses and gone home. Dexter, perceptive as always, had hung around, sensing this wasn't an ordinary evening in the life of Caroline Hills. She'd asked about his life growing up in Leicester, but hadn't yet volunteered many details about herself.

'Have you never wanted to live anywhere else?' she asked.

'Sometimes. I can see the appeal of getting out of the city, definitely. But it's where my friends are. My roots. Plus it's too bloody expensive to live anywhere else.'

Caroline smiled. 'Everything seems cheap to me,

compared to London. That's a city I was more than happy to get out of.'

'And now,' he said, chinking his glass against hers, 'we just have to get the city out of you.' After a few drinks, Caroline had to agree. 'So why were you so keen to leave? Just had enough of it?' he asked.

She sighed. 'Yeah, sort of. Lots of things going on at once. Mark's dad and brother both died within the past two years. Cancer. Josh had trouble with bullies at school. I was sick of dealing with knife murders, gangs and drugs. I came to realise it wasn't the sort of place I wanted to bring my kids up in. I didn't want them around London anymore, and I didn't particularly want myself around there either. One thing led to another, I started looking around and heard about the vacancy here.'

'Why Rutland?'

'Honestly? Because I'd never heard of it. We googled it and it looked nice, so we came to look at some houses. Bought the first one we looked at.'

'Blimey. You must've been keen to get out.'

Caroline shrugged. 'Maybe so. Life's a learning curve, eh? You staying for one last drink?'

Dexter looked at his empty glass, then back at Caroline. 'Yeah, go on then. Coke again, please. One last one. Then I've really got to go.'

She stood up, picked up the empty glasses and started to walk to the bar. And that was when she spotted Patrick Walsh.

17

Patrick Walsh looked exactly as he had in the photos, except clearly a few years older. He looked as though he'd tried to keep fit since retiring from professional rugby, but even he was unable to stop the barrage of passing time.

'It's Patrick, isn't it?' Caroline said, feeling far more confident and outgoing thanks to the alcohol.

'It is indeed. And to what do I owe the pleasure?' Walsh replied, evidently used to women talking to him in bars.

'I'm Caroline. I recognised you and wanted to say hi.'

'Ah. Tigers fan?'

'Oh yes,' she said, stoic on the outside but laughing inwardly to herself. 'Huge fan. Lifelong.'

'Glad to hear it! Not doing so well the past few years, mind. I'm not going to point out that it coincided with my retirement, but it definitely coincided with my retirement.' Walsh let out a huge belly laugh — enough to make a couple of punters in the saloon bar next door turn their heads.

Caroline didn't want to get boxed into a discussion about rugby — a sport she knew nothing about until very recently — and decided to change the subject.

'Did you hear about the murder over at Normanton?' she said.

Walsh narrowed his eyes. 'I did, yeah. Why'd you ask it like that?'

'Like what?'

'Ah. You're a copper, aren't you?'

'Guilty,' she said, raising her hands in mock salute, although she'd never intended to claim to be anything else. 'I'm working on the case, but I'm technically not on the clock right now. Still can't help myself from asking if anyone's heard anything, though. You know how it is.'

It wasn't the way Caroline had intended her first meeting with Patrick Walsh to go, but it seemed to be working in a strange way. Walsh was clearly uneasy, and that in itself was an advantage for Caroline.

'If you hear anything, get in touch, yeah?' she said, handing him her card. 'You can give me a call on that mobile number. Any time.' She added a wink for good measure. 'Ooh, while I remember, can I get a photo with you, please? I wasn't lying about the Tigers thing, I promise. I've been a fan ever since the Courage League win in 1988. First ever league champions, eh? They'll never take that away from us. I even got Rory Underwood's autograph that year.' She might not have been a rugby fan in the slightest, but she wasn't afraid to do her research when a potential suspect popped up on her radar.

'Yeah, course,' Walsh said, breaking into a smile.

Caroline waved Dexter over and handed him her phone. 'Can you get a photo of us, Dex? One for the scrapbook.'

'I've never understood that saying,' Walsh said. 'The word "scrapbook" always sounds a bit tatty and derogatory, doesn't it? I'm not sure I'd want to end up in anyone's scrapbook.' He laughed as he said it, making clear this was a lighthearted comment and not a serious request.

'Oh no,' Caroline said, feeling his tree trunk of an arm around her waist as she leaned in and smiled for the camera. 'I'll be keeping this picture very close at all times, don't you worry.'

18

When she woke up the next morning, Caroline didn't need to think back to how many drinks she'd had. She could feel every one of them. But despite the hangover, she felt good. She'd made two breakthroughs the previous evening: she'd connected with Dexter and finally opened up — at least partially — and she'd got the distinct sense that there was more to Patrick Walsh than met the eye.

She shouldn't have had a drink at all last night. A healthy body and a clear mind were vital today, and she was going into it with neither. She wasn't looking forward to it in the slightest. She never had done. But it was always fine when she got there, and it was something that needed doing.

She felt an incredible wave of guilt every time. She'd thought it might diminish after the first time or two, but it hadn't; it had got worse. She knew she'd have to tell Mark at some point. It was only a matter of time before he guessed or worked it out. But that wasn't something she was ready to do just yet.

She walked down the stairs like any other morning, dressed for work and trying to hide any emotion from her face. Mark was waiting in the kitchen.

'Morning,' he said. Caroline could hear the boys watching TV in the living room.

'Morning.'

'Good night?'

'Yeah. Made a nice change.'

There was still an undercurrent of frostiness after the previous morning, but Caroline didn't want to think about that. She had other things to focus her mind on. More worthy distractions.

'Good. It'd probably do you good to get out more,' Mark said. 'See people. Make friends.'

'They're work colleagues.'

Mark raised his hands in mock surrender. 'Alright. Just saying. It might help you loosen up a bit, that's all.'

'I don't need to "loosen up", Mark. I'm a forty-year-old woman with two kids, and I'm the Senior Investigating Officer in charge of a murder case. I'm not backpacking round Tibet on my gap year.'

'It's all relative. Quick pint in the pub, three weeks smacked off your tits on magic mushrooms. Although I don't think anyone could call last night a *quick* pint.'

'Oh, encouragement in one sentence and a reprimand in the next. How very caring.'

Mark chuckled. 'I'm not reprimanding you. I'm just pointing out you clearly had fun.'

'It was fine. I had one or two drinks with colleagues, then I came home.'

Mark took a sip of his coffee. 'What time did you get in?' he said, over the rim of the cup he was cradling.

'I dunno, I didn't look at the clock. Just after eleven, I think.'

'Try half twelve.'

'Try asking me questions you don't already know the answer to, Columbo.'

Mark smiled. 'Good job you're a copper. You'd be dreadful in the dock.'

'What's that meant to mean?' Caroline said, feeling her chest constrict and her voice tighten.

'Nothing. It was just a joke.'

'Well it's not a very funny one.'

'Alright, alright. Calm down. What's got into you this morning?'

'Nothing. I'm fine. Sorry. Just a headache.'

'What's the bag for, Mum?' Archie said, rounding the corner into the kitchen.

'Hmmm?'

'The bag by the front door.'

'Oh. Yeah, I was thinking about going to the gym after work. There's some new scheme they're doing. We get it half price with police ID. Thought I'd give it a go. Will see how I feel later.'

'A gym?' Mark asked. 'You've never set foot in a gym in your life.'

'All the more reason to start now, then, isn't there? Anyway, like I said, I might not bother. I'll see how I feel after work. Speaking of which,' she said, glancing at the clock on the kitchen wall, 'I should get going. I've got a meeting first thing.'

Even though he liked to think he was quite an easy-going guy, the last few months had been difficult for Mark.

He'd been far less attached to London than Caroline and the boys had been, and only lived within the M25 because it was convenient on the odd occasion he needed to visit clients in town. That had become rarer over the years, with emails and video-conferencing meaning it mattered very little where he lived. Their only links to London had been Caroline's work and the boys' schooling — both things which were easily moved.

When the time had come, it had proven remarkably easy to pull the trigger. It wasn't difficult to sell a house in North London at the best of times, and they'd actually found it much harder to decide where to move to. It had been Caroline's work which had dictated that, and the house in Oakham had appeared on Rightmove on the same day Caroline applied for the position of Detective Inspector with Rutland Police.

There was a definite undercurrent of unease, though. The family were settling into life in Rutland as well as could be expected, but Mark could tell Caroline wasn't happy. She'd lived in London all her life, and although he knew she'd find it difficult to adjust to a rural existence, he'd thought she would at least take solace in the positive impact it would have on Archie and Josh.

They both seemed much happier up here, and had made friends quickly. The change in Josh had been extraordinary, especially after the bullying he'd suffered in London. It had, without doubt, been the right decision to move. He just needed Caroline to realise that.

With the boys dropped off at school, Mark headed to the fridge to grab a bite to eat. As soon as he opened it, he noticed the distinctive white carrier bag on the middle shelf and sighed. He could tell Caroline had something on her mind that morning. She often did — but it was never usually enough to make her forget her lunch. Realising he could do with the walk anyway, he took the bag out of the fridge, slipped on his shoes and walked down Ashwell Road, towards the police station. It was a sunny day, and he'd reward himself by having a quick mooch around town and a bite to eat in one of the cafes before heading home to work.

As he reached the gates on Station Road, he saw a familiar figure walking to his car.

'Dexter!' he called, holding the white carrier bag up in the air.

Dexter walked over to him, only realising who he was once he was a few feet away. 'Oh! Mark, isn't it?'

'Yeah. We met a few weeks back. Sorry. I just wanted to

drop this in while I was walking past. It's Caroline's lunch. She left it in the fridge.'

'Oh right,' Dexter said, holding out a tentative hand.

'What?' There was a tone in Dexter's voice that made Mark feel uneasy.

'No, nothing. It's just… Well, she's not in today. Maybe there's been some confusion or something.'

'What do you mean she's not in?'

'She's got the day off. She's back tomorrow.'

'Day off? No, she said she was going to work. She made a packed lunch. She even had her bag for the gym, and said she was going to go after work.'

'Gym?' Dexter said, trying to stifle his laughter. 'Caroline? Are you sure you didn't dream all this?'

Mark swallowed and forced a smile. He very much hoped he had.

20

She always felt numb afterwards. The natural physiological response was to feel elated and exhilarated — almost as if her body was preparing her for the inevitable crash and burn — but it had since adapted into skipping that whole charade and going straight to sheer guilt and exhaustion. All she wanted in that moment was to open up and tell Mark, but she couldn't. She needed to protect him, protect the boys. The time would come when she'd have to open up and admit it, but she wasn't ready yet.

Back in her work clothes, she stepped into the house and walked straight through to the utility room, putting her casual clothes in the washing machine and setting the cycle. Mark knew Caroline wasn't exactly a gym bunny, but even that wouldn't explain her coming home with the clothes worn, but still clean.

'Good day?' he asked, appearing behind her.

'Yeah, not bad,' she said, forcing a smile.

'You left your lunch here.'

'Yeah, I know. Sorry.'

'It's in the fridge.'

'It'll keep for tomorrow.'

'You going in tomorrow?'

'Course I am. Why wouldn't I?'

'Just wondered. Dinner's nearly ready if you want to sort out the table.'

They ate in almost complete silence. Usually, she'd tell Josh off for playing with his Nintendo Switch at the table, but this time she didn't care. Archie was clearly cheesed off at something his brother had said or done, and was keeping quiet himself. With Mark offering no attempts at deep conversation, Caroline was secretly quite happy with the peace.

When dinner was finished, Mark cleared away the plates.

'Boys, do you want to go upstairs for a bit?' he asked. They didn't need telling twice, and bounded up to their rooms like puppies.

Caroline didn't know whether the tension was still left over from Mark's careless pregnancy remarks the previous morning or if there was something else she'd done wrong, but she didn't have the energy to challenge him.

'What's going on, Caz?' he asked, eventually.

'What do you mean?'

'With you. You've changed. What's wrong?'

'Nothing. I'm just tired and stressed. There's a lot going on at work.'

'How'd you know?'

'What do you mean?'

'You didn't go to work today.'

Caroline blinked. He'd said it with such conviction, there was no point in denying it.

'Why do you say that?'

'Because I went to drop off your lunch and they said you had the day off.'

Caroline sighed. 'No, I was out of town. We've got a lead in the case I'm working on. We've got to keep our powder dry and there are things we can't discuss.' It was wishy-washy enough to be convincing, but Caroline hated lying to Mark.

'What kind of lead?'

Caroline looked at him for a moment. 'I can't tell you that.'

'Yes you can. You don't have to be specific. But right now I'm honestly not believing a word of this. Something's going on, Caz. I know it is. And if you're not going to tell me what, then I think that says more than anything else.'

'There's nothing going on.' All she wanted to do was sleep.

'Look me in the eye and tell me everything's fine. Tell me you're not hiding anything.'

'Mark, can we just drop this please? I'm really tired.'

'Surely you've at least got the energy to tell me you're not keeping things from me?'

She swallowed hard. There was no easy way out of this. She didn't want to hide things from Mark, but above all else she needed to protect him. She was damned if she did and damned if she didn't. She raised her head and looked her loving husband in the eye.

'I'm not hiding anything,' she said.

21

After she arrived at work the next morning, Caroline asked Aidan Chilcott to take a closer look at the church. She wanted details on regular churchgoers, people involved on a voluntary basis and anyone who might have had a reason to want Roger Clifton dead. She felt sure the answer lay with Patrick Walsh, but there were still a few dots that needed connecting. Often, the best way to do that was under formal interview. Fortunately, she'd had the foresight to get his number before leaving. She knew there was little chance he'd get in contact with her, and she'd had a feeling she was going to need to get hold of him.

She called the number she'd saved in her mobile and called it from her office phone, which she knew would come up on Walsh's mobile as an unknown number.

'Hi, is that Patrick?' she asked when the call connected.

'Speaking.'

'Hi, Patrick. It's Detective Inspector Caroline Hills here

from Rutland Police. We met in the Wheatsheaf on Wednesday night.'

'Hi. How can I help?' Walsh replied, barely able to disguise the worry in his voice.

'I was wondering if you might be able to pop into our office on Station Road today for a quick chat. I just wanted to ask you a few questions.'

'Questions? What about?'

'We can go through all that when we meet. Are you free after lunch?'

'Well, no. I'm out of town today.'

'Alright. How about tomorrow?'

'Uh, well I'm helping out at the church fete. Is something the matter?'

Caroline jotted some notes down on the paper in front of her. There was the church connection — right from the horse's mouth. In trying to make himself sound like a good Christian, Walsh had inadvertently thrown himself in at the deep end.

'Oh no, nothing that can't wait a day or two,' she said. 'How's Sunday? I'm in the office in the morning if that helps?'

'Sunday? I'll be at church.'

Keep digging, Patrick, Caroline thought to herself. 'Okay. Monday?'

There was a pause at the other end of the line. 'I might be able to do that. I just need to check a few things. Can I call you back?'

'You can indeed. The number's on the business card.'

She knew Walsh wouldn't call her back. But he didn't

need to. She knew exactly what her next step was going to be.

Shortly after she put the phone down, there was a knock on her door. It was Dexter, and he had a huge, beaming smile on his face.

'You're not gonna believe this,' he said, rubbing his hands together. 'Me and Sara've been doing a bit of digging, if you'll pardon the pun.'

'What pun?'

'I'm getting there. So, Rutland Water was created in the early seventies when they built a dam and flooded the valley, right?'

'So you keep telling me.'

'I'll give you three guesses as to one of the construction companies that was involved in that work.'

Caroline slowly nodded. 'I'm pretty sure I can get this in one. Arthur Clifton Construction?'

'Ten points to DI Hills.'

'Do I win a speedboat?'

'Bad taste. Speaking of which, do you remember that guy Howard Smallwood who spoke to us at the boating centre? The guy wearing the frog jumper. I reckon we should give him a call. He's clearly barmy, but he's exactly the sort of guy who might have some juicy information.'

Caroline thought about this for a moment. 'Alright,' she said. 'Give him a call. But on one condition.'

'What's that?'

'Tell him not to wear that bloody frog jumper.'

22

Even Caroline had to admit that a four-minute walk down Church Street didn't warrant her starting up the car, parking a hundred yards down the road, paying for a ticket and then walking the rest of the way to Otters.

The cafe was bustling, as it was most mornings, but there was no mistaking Howard Smallwood. He looked just as Caroline might have expected the president of a local history society to look. He gave the impression of a cross between a supply teacher and a man eternally stuck in the past.

Caroline had heard colleagues and locals talk about Otters, but she'd never crossed the threshold. She realised now why the rest of town seemed so quiet each morning: because everyone was in here. She introduced Dexter and herself to Howard, adding two black coffees to the table's order.

'I understand my colleague's been in touch,' she said, giving Dexter the side-eye.

'That's right, yes. Some potential historical connection, you said?'

'Sort of,' Dexter replied. 'As I mentioned on the phone, we're a bit rusty on that front, so we wondered if you might be able to help.'

'I'll do my best,' Howard said, smiling. 'What is it you want to know?'

Dexter was keen not to tell him too much at this stage. It was generally a good idea to only let expert witnesses know as much as was necessary. Evidence would be much stronger if it came independently. 'Well, we're not really sure. We're clutching at straws a bit, if I'm honest. I was hoping you might have a bit more background and context than the standard history books and websites. Maybe we could start with the history of Rutland Water?'

One side of Howard's face curled up in a smile. 'How long have you got? I could write a book this thick about that,' he said, signalling a weighty tome with his hands. 'It changed the entire fabric of the county overnight. It divided the community. Families, even. We went from being a rural farming county to a tourist hotspot in the space of months. I've lived in Rutland all my life. I can remember what it was like back then. Hardly ever had anyone from outside come into the county. Nowadays, you'll be hard pushed to find a Rutlander in Rutland.' Caroline and Dexter shared a look, which Howard seemed to notice immediately. 'Oh. No, I didn't mean... Not in a racist way, I mean.'

'It's fine,' Dexter said. 'I'm from Leicester, anyway, so I didn't take it personally. You meant those dodgy London types, right?'

Howard smiled, pleased he'd managed to wriggle out of that one. 'Well, I think it'd be fair to say we wouldn't have places like this if we were still a county of farmers. I moan about it, but it's a great town to be an old duffer in nowadays.'

Dexter laughed. 'Have you always lived in Oakham, then?'

'No, only for the past fifteen years or so. Lived in a few of the villages in my time. Never outside the county, though.'

Caroline was no expert on local history, but even she knew that Rutland hadn't even existed as a county between 1974 and 1997. She would have put money on Howard Smallwood having point-blank refused to use the word "Leicestershire" in his address for those twenty-three years. 'Still, times change, eh?' she said, having a bit of fun with this. 'As you say, it wouldn't be sustainable now. At least it's all given the county a new lease of life.'

'Oh, indeed. The history society does as well as it does because of what Rutland is,' Howard said, as Caroline tried to make sense of those words through her pounding headache. 'Lots of people come here for Rutland Water and fall in love with the place. That means a lot more people who've got an interest in the history of the area. It's all about how you look at things, isn't it? I mean, to look at me now, you wouldn't think there's a lump the size of an olive pushing on my brain, ready to kill me at any moment, would you?'

'Uh, no,' Caroline said, looking at Dexter. 'No, that's not something I would have guessed. Sorry to hear that.' She wriggled slightly, trying to avoid the uncomfortable pause. 'So what happened when Rutland Water was created? Did they literally just dam the area off and flood it?'

'Oh no, they did "preparations",' Howard said, complete with air quotes. 'Although in reality all that meant is they knocked down everyone's houses and lined the valley with concrete. Even if you drained that entire bloody reservoir right now, you wouldn't get any of it back. Lost forever. You can't even imagine the uproar at the time. It was unbelievable. Makes that fiasco over the bloody McDonald's seem like a primary school protest.'

Rutland had, until recently, been the only county in England without a McDonald's — something which was on the verge of changing, after planning approval had been granted for a restaurant on the outskirts of Oakham. Despite Howard's belittling of the situation, Caroline felt sure he was exactly the sort of person who would have opposed it.

'So what was the basis for doing it? What was it all about?' she asked.

'Anglian Water needed more infrastructure. They own Rutland Water to this day. They turned it into a tourist hotspot too, with the boating, fishing, walks, bird spotting… the list goes on. It brings a huge number of tourists in, who spend money in hotels, restaurants, pubs and shops. Keeps the county busy and bustling. So, I presume this is all about the body that was found down at Normanton?'

'We can't comment on any specific cases,' she said.

'That's a yes, then. Listen, I know everyone round here.

If you need any help or information, just give me a call, alright? Always more than happy to help out.'

23

Caroline and Dexter left Otters, crossed the road and headed back up Church Street, towards the police station.

'You're still not convinced, are you?' Dexter said, recognising the look on his boss's face.

'About what?'

'That it's historical, somehow.'

'It just makes no sense. I mean, think about it. If it's linked with history in some way, why not do it back then? Most murders are committed when emotions run high, when feelings are fresh. It's a heat-of-the-moment thing.'

'I dunno. This seems pretty well planned and pre-meditated.'

'Yes, but fifty years' worth of planning? I think that's probably going a bit far. And again, it makes our killer a pensioner. From a practical point of view, if this is historic, why not do it before CCTV's widespread? And mobile phone tracking. Forensics, even. Every day the killer waited, their job got harder.'

'What if they didn't care?' Dexter said. 'What if they wanted to be caught? What if that was the whole point?'

'Then why the wild goose chase? If they wanted to be caught so badly, they could've hung around at the church with their hands in the air. Think about this logically. It makes no sense to wait until now, unless it's all based on something that happened recently. Roger Clifton was a local man. People knew him. His killer could have got to him at any point. So why now?'

'Roger might've been local, but maybe his killer wasn't. Maybe the motive is historical, but the means and opportunity only became apparent recently.'

Caroline shook her head. 'Doesn't make any sense. You don't just file a note away at the back of your mind to do a quick murder next time you're passing through Rutland.'

'You do if you *couldn't* get here before then, though.'

'How do you mean?'

'What if our killer's been in prison? Or out of the country?'

Caroline's jaw tensed as she considered this. 'That's a point. Call Sara and ask her if she's had any luck with the Spanish authorities in relation to Arthur Clifton. We'll need to build profiles on Roger's other connections, too. See if there's anyone who's been inside. I doubt you'll find anyone who's been banged up for fifty years, though. Wasn't the country's longest-serving prisoner let out a year or two ago? Even he'd only done forty-odd years. I can't help thinking this road doesn't go anywhere, Dex, no matter how many different ways you try.'

'Alright, so something more recent. A shady business

deal? Dodgy council business? Is that enough reason to kill someone?'

'Oh, Dex. You would've melted if you'd joined the Met. I once led a case into a woman who stabbed her husband to death because he used the veg chopping board to cut up meat.'

Dexter chuckled. 'To be fair, that's pretty dangerous.'

'So's ramming a steak knife into your husband's neck. Listen, what if we've got the symbolism all wrong? What if that's all just some nutter having a bit of fun? Maybe it was a business thing, or a council decision. Perhaps our killer is seriously unhinged and saw murder as justifiable. If they're that deranged, the whole symbolism of the church could've been their attempt to piss around. Send out a message, perhaps.'

'True. But it could also be someone very clever and calculating. Roger spent his life in construction and local politics. I think it's fair to say he will have ticked a few people off in his time. And there's a fine line between genius and insanity.'

'Who said that?' Caroline asked. 'Sounds like something Oscar Wilde would come out with.'

'Close. Oscar Levant. He was America's cross between Oscar Wilde and Noel Coward. "There's a fine line between genius and insanity. I have erased this line." That's the full quote.'

Caroline smiled and nodded, well aware that some lines had clearly been erased.

'Right,' she said as they arrived back on Station Road. 'Have you got an hour or two free?'

'Nothing that can't wait. Why?'

'Because I fancy something a little bit different. How do you fancy going to a church fete?'

Dexter had immediately clocked Caroline's thinly-veiled motivation. Despite her earlier comments, she was still convinced there was a religious background to Roger Clifton's murder, but he also knew she wasn't going to let it go. If nothing else, it was an hour out of the office and a chance to mingle with the locals. There was even a half-decent chance one or two of them might have some information that would be useful to them.

They parked up a little way down the road from the church, the streets already lined with cars — presumably due to people travelling from neighbouring villages to visit the church fete. By now, the sun was shining strongly and it was shaping up to be a beautiful day.

Caroline took stock of the happy faces, excited children and bunting that set the scene, and realised it was something that never would've happened in London. There were fetes and events, but they didn't quite have the same community feel she was seeing in front of her in that moment.

'Where do you stand on fudge?' Dexter asked, gesturing towards one of the stalls as they stepped into the church hall.

'I try not to,' Caroline said. 'Makes my shoes awfully sticky.'

'Shall we get a bag? I'm pretty sure it's the same guy that

was at the food and drink festival in Oakham last year. If it is, the coconut fudge is divine.'

'As long as you're not thinking of putting it on expenses,' Caroline replied, noticing he was already halfway to the stall.

Dexter beamed as he returned with the bag of bright pink fudge, looking like a child who'd just been rewarded for good behaviour. 'Oh, hello,' he said, a concerned tone in his voice.

'Not the same as last year?'

'No, over there.'

Caroline followed Dexter's eyes and looked over at the tombola stall. And there, slowly turning the colour of coconut fudge, was Patrick Walsh.

24

Caroline was keen not to spook Patrick by questioning him too heavily at the fete, but she did at least need to make her presence known. It was usually the case that first-time — and even some experienced — criminals had a tendency to change their behaviour, particularly once they knew the police were interested in them. For now, their job was to sit back and observe.

She was, though, more than a little intrigued by Patrick Walsh being so heavily involved in the church. While there was no rule against huge, burly-looking rugby players having a religious streak, something didn't quite sit right with Caroline. Before Dexter could say anything, Caroline walked over to greet Walsh.

'Hi!' she said, with forced jollity. 'Good turnout, isn't there?'

'Pretty good, yeah. Encouraging. Everyone's put a lot of work into this.'

She nodded, well aware of the slightly menacing tone to his voice. 'Do you tend to get involved with these sorts of events quite a lot, then?'

'Yeah, I do, as a matter of fact.'

'Committed Christian?'

'Devout.'

In that moment, Caroline realised why she'd felt so uncomfortable at the prospect of Patrick Walsh. The man was a walking contradiction. Friendly when drinking, cold when sober. A devout Christian, yet rumoured to be having an affair with a married woman. Working the tombola stall at a church fete, whilst still stinking of booze from the previous evening.

'I'm glad to hear it,' she said, looking him in the eye. 'Too many people tend to lose their moral fibre too easily these days.'

Caroline spotted the Reverend Peter Tottman on the other side of the room and wandered over to him. 'Thought we'd pop down to lend our support,' she said, introducing herself to the reverend's wife, Sheila. 'It certainly seems to be going well.'

'Yes, it's good to see the village in such good spirits,' Sheila said. 'Considering.'

'Well, it's a very British thing to be able to forget bad news when there's such divine fudge available, eh, Dex?'

Dexter smiled uncomfortably. 'Showing my support for local business,' he said.

Noticing the reverend had peeled off to speak to a couple of keen local parishioners and clearly intent on avoiding conversation with the police, Caroline decided to try to probe a little further with his wife.

'Have the locals been talking about it, then? Roger Clifton's death, I mean.'

'Oh, I should say. He used to live in the village, you know. His wife and daughter still do.'

'Was he popular?'

Sheila snorted. 'That's not the word I'd use. He certainly wasn't popular in the church, anyway. He always had a bad word to say about everybody. His wife has been quite involved in the church over the years, but it was almost as if he was opposed to it somehow.'

'Oh?'

'Well, look. We're well aware most people aren't religious. And those that are probably aren't Christians. And those that are probably aren't Methodists. That's fine. But Roger always tried to get in little digs and barbs. He couldn't just be non-religious. He had to actively undermine everything we did or said.'

'Like what?' Caroline asked.

Sheila let out a sigh. 'Oh, all sorts. There was one time, back when he still lived here, we had an evening soiree. All sounds very la-di-da, I know, but really it was just a chance to open the church, raise some money and drink prosecco with a few nibbles. Roger had clearly been in the pub since lunchtime, and had come looking for Alice. Peter told him she'd already gone home, and he started ranting and raving, saying he knew she was here somewhere. She wasn't, though. She'd started to feel a bit ill about an hour in and had gone home to bed. But

Roger wouldn't take no for an answer. He was going off on one, shouting about how the church had got in the way of their marriage, was taking up all her time, how it was all a load of old nonsense anyway. Peter stepped in and tried to defuse the situation, and Roger started yelling at him too.'

'Oh dear. That doesn't sound very nice.'

'No, not at all.'

'How did it end?'

'A few of the chaps stepped in and threw him out.'

'Do you remember who?'

'If my memory serves me correctly, I think it was Tim, John and Patrick. Why?'

'I just wondered. I imagine quite a few people will have been upset.'

'Not enough to murder him, if that's what you're thinking. We don't get quite *that* protective over our religion.'

'No, I didn't mean that. Sorry,' Caroline said.

'Ah. Hang on. Are you the two detectives who came to speak to Peter yesterday?'

There was no way Caroline could wriggle out of this one. 'We are. We wanted to come and apologise, actually.'

'Don't worry, I know you were just doing your job,' Sheila said, almost conspiratorially. 'Between you and me, I think Peter's been quite rattled by the whole thing. He's been trying to keep the peace for a long time, and it's been quite upsetting for him to see it come to a head like this.'

All of a sudden, Caroline got the distinct impression there was far more to this than a simple row over theology. 'What do you mean, Mrs Tottman?' she asked.

Before Sheila could respond, her eye was taken by the

returning reverend, who'd taken this moment to rejoin the group.

'It's good to see you again, Detective Inspector,' he said, smiling. 'I received your apology from Chief Superintendent Arnold. Thank you for that. Humility is a great virtue.'

Caroline forced a smile, but inside she was seething.

25

That evening, Caroline struggled to relax. She was having trouble focusing her mind on any one thing right now, and that was a major problem. Being the Senior Investigating Officer on a murder investigation was no small task, and required full attention at all times. But then so did a lot of other things in her life right now.

Mark, to his credit, seemed to have taken her words the previous evening to heart. He'd seemed genuinely pacified when she looked him in the eye and told him she wasn't keeping any secrets. She, on the other hand, felt dreadful for her lies. But her concern right now wasn't for herself.

She'd come home that day to find a selection of snacks and drinks waiting for her in the 'fun' fridge, as they called it, in the garage. Mark had been into town and stocked up on treats from a few of the local independent shops, as well as some Grainstore ciders — a special treat for a warm evening. Fortunately for Caroline, she felt able to stomach cider that evening. Red wine was still very much off the cards.

She'd tried to engage with the boys after work, and listened intently as Archie and Josh told her about their days at school — Archie more passionately than Josh, but Josh was already fast becoming a teenager before his years.

A part of her wondered whether she'd been wrong to take on the case. She couldn't even keep a coherent and related string of thoughts, so how could she give her all to a murder investigation? She felt she'd lost her direction. She'd gone so far down the path of the religious motive, and she was now left questioning its validity. She'd honed in on Patrick Walsh, not enough to find any evidence or reason to arrest him, but just enough to spook him and allow him to potentially cover his tracks.

That had been her biggest worry. Timing was often the most important aspect of any police investigation. The first twenty-four hours were often known as the 'golden period'. Major progress within that time period greatly increased the chances of success. But once the first twenty-four hours were over, success rates fell off a cliff. The timing of arrests needed to be carefully done, too. Whilst it was true they could arrest anyone without real reason — and many Senior Investigating Officers considered this to be beneficial as it meant statements made by the arrested person were admissible in court under the Police and Criminal Evidence Act — Caroline took a more cautious approach. She'd learned from experience that moving too quickly could be as dangerous as moving too slowly, especially if a suspect was arrested, then released because of a lack of evidence at the end of their twenty-four-hour custody period, only to then go missing or commit further crimes.

These sorts of decisions were second nature to her. They weren't something she ever really thought about — not consciously, anyway. It was almost reflexive. But now, for the first time in many years, she found herself thinking more strategically and carefully about it. It was as if the instincts had gone, the automatic reflexive decisions weren't firing and she had to actually think things through.

When she'd taken on the case, she'd felt as if she was towering above it, able to look down and see what needed doing, what course needed to be charted. And now she was halfway down the river, floating in the wrong direction having totally misjudged the currents, without a paddle and with utter confusion reigning free inside her mind.

It wasn't a feeling she was familiar with. She was used to being in control, having full confidence and feeling comfortable in her job. But this felt very different. Now, for the first time in her career — although not in her life — she felt confused and completely alone.

26

Caroline had always tried to ensure that Sundays were relaxing family days. The nature of police work meant that was far from guaranteed, particularly if shift work was necessary, but that was thankfully rare in Rutland CID.

She didn't know if it was just tiredness, but she detected a different atmosphere from usual as Josh and Archie ate their breakfast. The boys were fine — the frostiness seemed to come from Mark. She guessed she shouldn't be surprised. They hadn't exactly been close lately, which she recognised but felt powerless to do much about. The further they drifted apart, the harder it was to open up and communicate.

As a couple, they'd always "got" each other. It was more of an unspoken understanding than anything else, and there'd never been the need for emotional heart-to-hearts or long, in-depth chats. The bedrock of their relationship had been that intense closeness which had meant they didn't *need* to talk, but the advent of children had slowly eroded that closeness away until they'd been left with a perfectly functional and happy relationship, but one in which Caroline didn't feel she was able to open up, even when she needed to.

It had certainly been far less eventful than the previous Sunday, and part of her felt slightly uneasy at having the day off. She was perfectly entitled to it, but she felt her presence would be much more welcome and needed at work than it was at home. Mark was reading a magazine on the sofa, the boys were playing in the garden and she was milling around, tidying up and doing very little. Rest days were important, but she didn't half feel guilty when they came around.

The concept of a 'rest' day was almost laughable to her. Even if she could entomb herself for six months and hibernate, she was pretty sure she wouldn't emerge feeling rested. It was an intense, long-term exhaustion which couldn't be cured by a day off spent rearranging the teabags.

'Dad, can you come and play football with us?' Archie asked, poking his head through the gap in the patio doors.

'Yeah, in a bit. Let me just finish this.'

'Mark, you're reading a magazine,' Caroline said, watching as Archie moped back towards his brother on the lawn.

'Yeah, and I'm not just going to stop in the middle of an article because someone demanded it. He didn't even say please.'

'He's six.'

'Exactly. He should have some manners by now. Why

don't you go and kick a ball around with them? You're not doing much. I'll be out in a bit.'

'I'm on a rest day, Mark. You're the one who said I work too much and need to relax.'

'Alright, calm down. What's this all about?'

'What's what all about? I'm just saying put a bookmark in the fucking magazine and go and play football with your son, alright?'

Mark closed the magazine and slid it onto the coffee table.

'What's the matter, Caz?'

'Nothing. I'm fine.'

'You're not fine. You're snappy. You don't look good.'

'Oh, thanks.'

'You look pale. Exhausted.'

'Yeah, you can leave it there, thanks, Mark.'

'Alright. Alright. I'll leave you to it.'

She watched as he stepped out into the garden and jogged across the lawn, listening to the shrieks of delight from Archie as their football team was complete.

The rest of the day passed without note. Caroline tried to keep away from Mark and the boys as much as possible. She knew she wouldn't be much good to them in her current frame of mind, and was likely to wind Mark up further. Still, it wouldn't be long before she could get back to normal. Once the case was closed and passed on to the CPS, much of the stress would be lifted. And her meeting on Thursday morning would — she hoped — put one particular chapter of her life to bed, once and for all.

It was something she hadn't told Mark. A secret she'd kept from him. Another one. But she'd had good reasons. She always had good reasons. Everything she did, everything she said, everything she didn't say — it was all to protect Mark and the boys. She'd never wanted anything else, and she was unwavering in that.

There were some couples and families who believed you couldn't truly be close unless you knew absolutely everything about a person. But Caroline knew that wasn't true. She recognised that true closeness came when you didn't *need* to know everything about another person because you loved, knew and accepted them anyway. She'd never been a fan of drama; she didn't need the spotlight shining on her. She just got on with things. She'd rarely seen the need to sit down and waste time talking about something when she could be actively fixing it and getting it sorted instead.

By the time the evening had rolled round and the boys were in bed, she'd resolved to spend a couple of hours watching a film with Mark. That had been easier said than done. Although she was trying her hardest to focus on the screen and follow the storyline, her mind kept wandering.

She pulled out her phone and opened the Photos app before bringing up the picture Dexter had taken the other night in the Wheatsheaf. She looked at the image, deep into the eyes of Patrick Walsh and silently asked him what he was hiding. There was something about the man that made her feel very uneasy, but she couldn't quite put her finger on it. She'd get there eventually — she knew she would — but so far it was eluding her.

'You okay?' Mark asked, not taking his eyes off the television.

'Yeah. Fine.'

'Want a top-up?' he said, gesturing towards her empty glass on the coffee table in front of them.

Caroline put her phone down on the arm of the sofa. 'Yeah. Good idea,' she said. 'I'll get them.'

She stood up and walked to the kitchen with the empty glasses, a thousand thoughts running through her head. Sooner or later — somehow — she needed to find a way of organising them. Because otherwise she was in real danger of becoming a liability to herself, not to mention everybody else.

Caroline was no more a fan of Mondays than anyone else, but this one signified a fresh start. She was determined to make this week her week, and it was going to start with Patrick Walsh.

Walsh had finally agreed to come in and speak to Caroline in a voluntary interview. She was keen to stress to him that he wasn't under arrest, but she knew she could play that card at any time that suited her.

He arrived shortly after ten o'clock — something which riled Caroline straight away. So far as she could see, he had no reason to be late and she was certain he'd only done it as a power play. They sat down in the interview room — a far more formal setting than Caroline would've liked in this instance, but it was all they had.

Having settled Walsh in with a cup of tea, Caroline started with some gentle, casual questioning as Dexter sat next to her and took notes.

'So what's your connection with the Clifton family?' she asked, starting to move things on.

'How do you mean?'

'Well, how do you know them? How often do you see them? On what grounds? That sort of thing.'

'I met Alice through the church. I see them through the church. That's about it.'

'You don't see each other socially outside the church?'

'Sometimes, yeah.'

'What about Roger?'

'What about him?'

'Were you friendly with him?'

'I'm friendly with everyone.'

'How friendly are you with Alice Clifton?'

'Well, Roger asked me to keep an eye on her and support her while he was away travelling. I kept in touch with her, checked in on them occasionally. That sort of thing.'

'He asked you to do that?'

'Yeah.'

'Sounds to me like you and Roger were pretty close friends, then,' Caroline said, knowing full well from what the reverend had told them that this wasn't the case.

Patrick shrugged. 'Maybe it's a church thing. If you're in that circle, you tend to trust other people who are too. We Christians tend to be pretty trusting and forgiving.'

Caroline nodded slowly. 'You make quite a lot of your faith, don't you?'

'How do you mean?'

'You seem to mention it at every given opportunity. Almost as if it's a handy get-out clause for you. You couldn't possibly be guilty of anything, because you're a Christian. Is that it?'

He looked between the two of them. 'Sorry, am I under suspicion or arrest or something? I was told this was an informal chat.'

'It is. We can make it formal if you'd prefer.' Walsh stayed silent. 'Would you say religion is an important part of your life?' Caroline asked.

'I would, yeah.'

'How important?'

'Very.'

'Would you have said Roger was a religious man?'

'Not particularly, no.'

'Tell me more.'

'What more do you want to know? He wasn't particularly religious.'

'What, so he was silent on the matter? Didn't get involved? Loudly opposed it? What?'

'It just wasn't really his thing. That was his choice.'

'Were there ever any disagreements over it? Did he ever, perhaps, get a bit vocal in his opposition to it? Did he cause any issues at all?'

Walsh seemed to think about this for a few moments. 'I dunno. Possibly. I don't really remember.'

'You don't remember? You've got no memory of whether or not a man — someone you were close enough to to be trusted to look after the welfare of his family while he was away — at any point, at any time, kicked off and caused major disruption over his views on religion, something which plays a major part in your life?'

Walsh shrugged. 'People disagree and fall out all the time.'

'Did you fall out with Roger Clifton?'

'I didn't say that.'

'No, I did. Did you fall out with him?'

'Not particularly, no.'

'Not particularly?'

Walsh sighed. 'Look, if you think something happened that I've forgotten about, I'd appreciate it if you could let me know the details and see if it jogs my memory. To be honest, I don't like the way you're behaving. This was meant to be an informal chat, something to help you guys out and find out who killed Roger. But instead you've subjected me to some sort of Stasi interrogation. If you want to arrest me, arrest me. I'll call my lawyer and we'll go down that road. Otherwise, if it's quite alright with you, I'm going home.'

Caroline and Dexter left the interview room feeling they'd got no further in the investigation. If anything, it felt as though they'd gone backwards. They made their way back to the incident room and Caroline sat down at her desk before Sara Henshaw came bounding up with far more enthusiasm than Caroline felt.

'Good news, boss,' Sara said. 'We've been analysing Roger Clifton's laptop. I think we might have a pretty strong lead.'

'Go on,' Caroline said, her interest piqued.

'It's all pretty normal and above board, except for one thing. Someone sent Roger a threatening email almost exactly a week before he died.'

'What kind of threatening email?'

'I'll read it to you. "How do you sleep at night? You'll pay for your family's actions one way or another. Scum like you deserve to rot in hell."'

'Is that it?'

'Yep.'

Caroline exhaled. The religious connotations of "rot in hell" were too many for her to ignore, but now wasn't the time to push that particular angle again. 'Are we able to trace it?'

'Not me personally, but yes. The originating IP address was Oakham Library.'

'Wow. Okay. And we have the date and time it was sent, yes?'

'Yep.'

'Then we need to request CCTV footage from the library. At the very least, we'll be able to narrow it down to people we know were inside the library at the time.'

'Already done. They're going to pull the footage and get back to us.'

'Who are? The council?' Caroline asked. Sara nodded in return, and Caroline filed this away in her mind. Roger's links to the council were worth remembering.

'There's a slim chance they could narrow it down to the specific machine at their end, but they didn't make any promises. The computers aren't particularly top of the range, and anyone with a bit of knowhow could mask things fairly easily. But if they had that much knowhow they'd have used a VPN and not risked getting caught on CCTV.'

'Sorry. Acronym overload, Sara.'

'Virtual Private Network. Basically, every computer has an IP address. That's its position on the internet, if you like. Now, with a VPN, rather than me sending you an email and it bouncing from my machine to yours, it goes via dozens of other computers on the way, making the location of the original sender impossible to work out. You can usually only see the IP address of the last machine involved, which won't be the one the email was actually sent from.'

'Right. And the library's IP address could be that last machine involved? Bit of a coincidence, isn't it?'

'Yeah, absolutely. We don't think that's the case. But there's still a chance the sender wasn't even in the library.'

'What? How?'

'They could've got onto the network from outside. Could be as simple as connecting to the wifi from a car parked up by the building. We won't know until the CCTV comes back.'

Caroline nodded and thanked her. Sara was always one step ahead, constantly on the ball. At a time when it seemed the investigation was finally getting its first real breakthrough, colleagues like Sara were gold dust.

28

The wait for the CCTV footage from the library seemed interminable. For all Rutland's differences compared to London, it seemed they had one thing in common: waiting for councils to act.

Caroline felt surer than ever that Patrick Walsh was their man. She'd come across enough shifty people in her time to know when someone was playing her and trying to hide something. And although that wasn't enough in itself, as far as she was concerned there was more than enough linking him to Roger Clifton's murder.

Even more frustratingly, someone appeared to have replaced the coffee granules in the kitchenette with a different brand. She sipped the murky brown liquid, trying to ignore the taste and focus on the caffeine hit, when Sara Henshaw came in.

'Sara, you're smiling. Please tell me it's because the CCTV footage has come back, and not because you've got shares in whoever makes this godawful piss.'

'Wrong on both counts. But it's either going to throw us a massive bone or put an even bigger spanner in the works. Remember Roger Clifton's brother, who lives in Spain? The present-day Arthur. He's back.'

'Back? In the UK?'

'In Rutland. It looks like he's going to inherit the company. Apparently, there was a cloak and dagger meeting with a solicitor earlier this morning. Alice Clifton got wind of it and phoned the police. She was going apeshit, apparently, screaming that Arthur had killed Roger to get control of the company.'

'On what basis? He wasn't a shareholder or director, was he?'

'Something to do with the will. Reading between the lines, Roger had cut Alice out of it and there was some sort of extra documentation leaving the business to Arthur.'

'Christ. Okay, well that gives him a motive. Means and opportunity, not so much. Bit difficult to kill someone who's in another country.'

'Could have hired someone to do it.'

'Then turn up within a few days to claim the money? Something doesn't feel right there.'

She opened her office door and called over to Dexter. He stood up and walked towards them.

'Got a little job for you, Dex. Can you pop over to Alice Clifton's in Empingham and speak to her please? It looks like Roger's brother's back on the scene. We've had a call from her, kicking off about some secret meeting between Arthur and a solicitor over him inheriting the company.'

Dexter cocked his head and raised an eyebrow. 'Right, I see.'

'I know what you're thinking. Don't. These things happen all the time when people die. There's always someone who crawls out of the woodwork wanting money. It's rarely a reason for murder.'

'Could be a starting point, though.'

'It could. But we're a small team and we need to make sure we always focus on our strongest line of inquiry. We don't have the resources to be doing a full-on Sherlock Holmes reconstruction of every player's movements and motives. We're police officers. We look at the evidence and work backwards from there.'

As she said this, she realised how hypocritical it could sound. Had she really focused too heavily on Patrick Walsh and the religious aspect? No. Definitely not. The religious connections were clear and there for all to see. And Walsh's links were numerous. He'd been having his way with Roger Clifton's wife, was known to have had violent disagreements with Roger and had been acting suspiciously. He also fitted perfectly into the religious connection.

'Alright,' Dex said, clearly not in the mood for a disagreement. 'Anything else?'

Caroline shook her head. 'No, that'll be all,' she muttered.

29

Caroline arrived home that evening feeling as though she'd been hit by a ton of bricks. Mark had forgotten to switch the outside lights on — odd, as he was always the one reminding her to switch them on, then off again in the morning. It was on his to-do list to wire light sensors into them so they'd go off and on automatically with sunrise and sunset, but he hadn't got round to it yet. Still, it was unlike him to forget to switch them on.

There was a light on in the living room — the distant glow of the sideboard lamp, accentuated with the flickering colours of the television, which played off the walls.

She switched off her engine, grabbed her bag and got out of the car. She was sure this place would feel like home at some point. It was much bigger than the place they'd had in London, and had left them money in the bank. It was a lovely house — no doubt about it — but she didn't yet feel that connection, the sense of returning where she belonged.

She wondered how much of that Mark felt, too. It would go some way to explaining the frosty atmosphere around the place. She wasn't blameless in that regard, but she wasn't about to take full responsibility either.

Her instinctive reaction was to believe things had been simpler in London. But had they really? There'd still been other complications, but they were largely different ones. Still, she'd been able to be honest. She'd been open — at least with Mark. And she hadn't had to feel the guilt of holding back. At least, that's what was on the surface. That's what she could tell herself. It was safer than facing the truth. Safer than admitting — to herself — all of the secrets and things she'd been hiding. Suppressing. She'd hoped the move to Rutland would give her the fresh start she needed. She'd had visions of feeling freer, more able to open up and release herself from everything that had been holding her back. Time hadn't helped, and she'd banked everything on physical distance. So far, at least, one hundred miles didn't seem to be cutting it.

The truth followed her everywhere. She swallowed hard as the realisation struck her that she could never escape it, because escape wasn't possible. You can't escape what's inside you. It comes with you, wherever you go, spreading its trail of destruction further. Sooner or later she was going to have to face up to that.

She stepped into the house and closed the door behind her. She could see Mark in the living room, but he hadn't called out to her in his usual way. Even though they hadn't made eye contact or said a word to each other, the atmosphere was clear. She put her bag down and walked into the living room, keen to clear the air in the simplest, most painless way possible.

'Alright?' she said, sitting down on the sofa.

'Where've you been?' Mark asked, not taking his eyes off the screen.

'You know where I've been. I've been at work.'

'I know where you said you were going to be, yeah.'

'Oh come on, Mark. We've been through this. I can't give you every detail of my schedule, especially not when I'm on a major case. You know why I had to bend the truth the other day.'

'So why didn't Dexter tell me that? He specifically said you had the day off. He would've known that I knew that wasn't true. He would've said something along the lines of not being able to say anything, maybe a little white lie in telling me he wasn't sure where you were but he'd check and get you to give me a call. But no, he said you weren't in that day.'

'I wasn't. I was out of town. I told you that.'

'This isn't a game of word play, Caz.' There was a moment of silence before Mark spoke again. 'Who's the guy in the photo?'

'What guy?'

'There's a photo of you with your arm round some guy in the pub on Wednesday night. The night you got home late.'

'Where did you get that idea from?'

'It's on your phone. You left it unlocked last night when you went to get a drink. It was right there on the screen.'

Caroline closed her eyes. Her brain hadn't been

functioning properly for a while, and yesterday was when she'd started to really feel the tiredness kicking in. In her defence, there hadn't been anything to hide. Walsh was a witness at best, suspect at worst. She had no reason to keep the photo from Mark, but she knew exactly how he'd react if he saw it, and now she'd been proven right.

'You shouldn't have been looking. You're meant to trust me. And if you must know, he's a suspect in the case I'm working on. But you didn't hear that from me.'

'I'm meant to believe that, am I? You're having midweek drinks, smiles and hugs with a suspect?'

Caroline sighed. 'Mark, I'm really tired. There's a lot more to it than that. At the moment he's a sort of witness, but we're trying to get close to him to get more information.'

'Yeah. Very close, by the looks of things.'

'Look, it's policing. There's a lot of stuff I can't talk about and a lot of strategies that probably don't make sense if you're not involved.'

'And cuddling up to your suspects in the pub is one of them?'

'I wasn't cuddling up to him. He used to be a professional rugby player, I pretended I was a supporter and wanted a photo. What you're seeing there is me doing a bloody good job, might I add, of being an enthusiastic fan of his and nothing else. What, did you think I was having an affair and getting people to take photos of us together in public? Is that really what you take me for?'

'Caz, I don't know what to think anymore. You've changed so much recently.'

'Mark. Please. I'm so tired. I'm exhausted. I'm not doing this right now. All you need to know is I'm not having an affair, alright? Not with that bloke, not with anyone. I'm going to bed.'

30

Far from feeling refreshed after a night's sleep, Caroline somehow woke even more drained than she had been the night before. She'd planned to head out and speak to Arthur Clifton, but didn't feel she had the physical or mental energy to deal with it. The easiest and most sensible option would've been to send someone else, but that wasn't an option. Caroline liked to see the whites of people's eyes for herself.

She headed to the office's kitchenette and made herself the closest thing to a double espresso she could muster — two teaspoons of coffee granules and a couple of splashes of hot water. She downed it in one go, then made herself a full cup of strong coffee. Before she'd finished, Derek Arnold poked his head around the corner.

'Ah, Caroline. Can I have a quick word if you've got a sec, please?'

'Yeah, course. Here, or…?' She had a feeling she knew what the answer would be, and that she was about to find herself called into the Chief Superintendent's office for the second time in a week.

She was right, and followed Arnold back to his office, clutching her hot mug of coffee. She sipped at it as Arnold spoke, now safe behind the comfort of his desk.

'I've had another complaint from Reverend Peter Tottman,' he said, folding his arms.

'An official one? Or another little word in your ear?'

'He says you were harassing his wife at the Empingham church fete.'

'Harassing? Is that his word or yours?'

'His.'

'Right. Well obviously that isn't the case. We were in the same room as each other, so naturally we spoke.'

'What were you doing there?'

Caroline shrugged. 'It's a local church fete. I live locally, I decided to go along.'

'With DS Antoine? On work duty?'

'We were passing. There's a line of inquiry we're following up at present, which put a person of interest there, so we went along to observe and keep our ears to the ground.'

'Who's your person of interest?'

'I'd rather keep that close to my chest for now, for operational reasons.'

'Is the person a registered informant?'

'No sir.'

'I see. So are you going to tell me who it is?'

Caroline knew she had to have a watertight reason not

to tell him. Procedurally, she was out of her depth. If she refused, she'd be off the case.

'Patrick Walsh. The rugby player. We knew he'd be at the fete, so we went along to have an informal chat. When we got there we bumped into the reverend and his wife, so we got talking. That's it.'

'In that case, I'm going to have to formally request that any interviews, whether with suspects or witnesses, are done through the proper channels. This is a murder investigation. We've got to dot the i's and cross the t's. No more off-the-record chats, no prancing about at village fetes. The next time I pull you into this office, it'll either be to congratulate you for securing a charge, or to pull you off the case completely and hand it over to EMSOU. Do I make myself clear?'

Caroline tensed her jaw. 'Yes, sir. Perfectly clear.'

She stood and left Arnold's office and headed back to the incident room. Before she could reach the door, she started to feel lightheaded.

Her vision seemed to close in on itself, dark edges appearing around the outside, as if she was reversing at speed through a tunnel. A wave of nausea flooded through her, followed by a sudden hot flush. It was as though someone had turned the temperature up twenty degrees in an instant. Before she could work out what was going on, she felt her legs buckle beneath her. Trying desperately to steady herself against the wall, she slid down it, feeling the cold of the plaster against her back before the taste of iron in her mouth as she hit the floor and felt the world close in on her.

· · ·

It felt as though she'd blinked. Her breathing was shallow and she could feel the beads of sweat running down her face as she struggled to sit up.

'Alright, it's alright,' came the sound of Aidan's familiar voice. 'Let's take it easy. Take small sips of this for me.'

Caroline grasped the tumbler of water with shaking hands and did as he said. She felt weaker than she ever had before, and a thousand times as vulnerable.

'I'm fine. Don't worry,' she said. 'I shouldn't have skipped breakfast and lunch. I didn't get much sleep either.'

'Sara's called you an ambulance. They're on their way.'

'No. No. Cancel it. I'm fine. Please.'

'At least let me take you in. You need to be checked,' Sara said.

'No. I don't. I haven't eaten, I haven't slept. That's all. There's no point wasting their time. I just passed out, that's all.' She looked up at Aidan and Sara. 'Seriously. Cancel it. I'm not joking.'

Sara looked at Dexter. He gave a slight nod, and Sara walked away, mobile phone in hand.

'Aidan, go and get another glass of water, will you?' Dexter said, before watching him head towards the kitchenette. 'You alright?' he asked her.

'I'm fine, Dex. Honestly.'

'You don't look fine. What's been going on?'

'Nothing. I'm just tired and I haven't eaten.'

'You know I don't believe you, right?'

'I didn't ask you to.'

'We should probably hand this case over. I don't want to

any more than you do, but we're well out of our depth. If it's having this effect on you, we can't risk it.'

'It's not. The case is fine. I'm probably just coming down with something. It doesn't mean we have to give in and let the big boys run the show.'

'It's not about giving in. It's about knowing our limits and doing what's best for everyone. For Roger Clifton.'

By now, they could hear Aidan starting to return with the glass of water.

'No, Dex. It's not happening. I need your help and support right now. If you breathe a word of this to anyone, I'll never forgive you.'

31

'Pull over here. I'll take it the rest of the way.'

Dexter gave Caroline the side-eye. 'I think it'd be best if I drop you back at yours. You're still not right. I wouldn't feel comfortable with you driving.'

'I'm fine. You're overreacting. Anyway, I'll be home in thirty seconds.'

Dexter pulled over, bumping the car up onto the pavement on Ashwell Road. 'Mark home?'

'I imagine so.'

'You going to tell him about what happened?'

'Why, are you planning to check up on me?'

'No, I just think he has a right to know, that's all.'

'And what makes you think he won't?'

Dexter pointed at the road in front of them. Caroline sighed.

'I'll take it from here, Dex. Thanks for dropping me this far.'

'Alright. You're the boss,' he said, climbing out of the

driver's seat of Caroline's car and walking round onto the pavement. 'Listen. Before we speak to Arthur Clifton tomorrow, I just wanted to say something. I know you think there's something there with the family, or that there's some religious aspect. And yeah, there might be. But something Howard Smallwood said the other day made me think.'

'About?'

'About history. I've been doing a lot of reading up about it all, and it kind of makes sense. What if the church and everything else *is* religious symbolism, but not in the way we thought?'

'Sorry, Dex. You're going to need to start again and assume I've spent a portion of the day unconscious.'

'The working theory is that the symbolism is meant to represent Roger Clifton being a vocal atheist, and therefore the killer being a Christian, right?'

'Right.'

'But what if that's not it at all? What if the symbolism of the church — Normanton Church specifically — is that it *used* to be a church?'

'Dex, when I said dumb it down a bit…'

'Alright, alright. So fifty years ago a bunch of families were displaced from their homes, yeah? They'd probably lived there for generations, tended the land, been part of the community. Then a big company comes in and decides to flood the lot. That'd fuck you up good and proper.'

'Is that the official psychiatric term?'

'Don't forget the reason Normanton Church got deconsecrated was because of the flooding of the villages and the creation of Rutland Water. Otherwise, it'd still be a totally normal church on top of a hill, rather than a tourist attraction halfway underwater. Some of the families who lost their homes probably would've gone to that church.'

'What, you think someone's held a grudge for fifty years? And if that's the case, why Roger Clifton? He was only a kid when all that happened. He's hardly responsible for it, is he? Anyone who was involved is going to be long gone now. And anyway, attitudes have mellowed. Everyone knows it was for the best. The county's booming now.'

'Yeah, but what if they haven't mellowed? What if someone's been sitting there with it brooding for fifty years?'

'Then why now? And why Roger?'

Dexter sighed. 'I dunno. But we're close. I'm sure of it. There's got to be something we're missing. I can feel it.'

Caroline looked at him. 'Is that an admission that gut feelings are alright now, then? When they're your gut feelings, I mean.'

'No, I didn't mean it like that. If I'm right, the religious thing might have more legs than I thought. But I don't think it's the motive in itself. We'll get there. Just thought it was something worth mentioning. Maybe we might be able to put our heads together on it tomorrow.'

'Yeah. Tomorrow.'

'Perhaps Arthur Clifton'll be able to shed some light on things. Alice seems convinced he's been after the company for a while. Either way, I think we're getting closer than you reckon. These things don't take much. Only needs someone to slip something into conversation or make one wrong move, and we're in.'

'Thanks for covering for me, Dex. And thanks for dropping me home.'

'Most of the way home. Get some rest. I'll see you in the morning. We'll get this figured out, alright?'

Caroline nodded. 'I know we will.'

She got into the car and watched as Dexter walked back down Ashwell Road towards the town. She sighed heavily and rested her forearms on the steering wheel. Today had been an absolute disaster, in so many ways. She'd be glad to put it behind her. She hoped her weak excuse about not having eaten would wash with the team. The last thing she wanted was for anyone to feel she was weak or incapable. She'd got used to that being at the back of her own mind for too long — she certainly didn't need anyone else thinking it.

She bumped the car back down the kerb and accelerated away, looking forward to a good night's sleep.

32

Sleep, though, was hard to come by. It seemed that every step she took, the further she strayed from catching Roger Clifton's killer. Whichever direction she turned, she found resistance and ran into roadblocks.

It was the most frustrating case she'd worked on in a long time. All of the ingredients were there, but it seemed impossible to stitch everything together in a way that formed a coherent case. There were still too many holes, too many inconsistencies, too many places in which this could easily fall apart.

Patrick Walsh seemed, to her, to be a lead worth pursuing. The affair with Alice Clifton seemed all too convenient, but it seemed she didn't stand to make any benefit from Roger being dead. She already had the house, their separation had been amicable and she had no share in Arthur Clifton Construction. Then again, Alice Clifton's reaction when she found out Arthur was going to inherit the business made it clear she'd at least suspected she might be first in line. But was it strong enough?

The missing link seemed to be the younger Arthur. She didn't know what part he played, but his appearance back on the scene so soon after his brother's death couldn't be ignored. He had one thing, if nothing else: a motive.

The issue was that he wasn't in the country when Roger died. There was, of course, always the possibility that he could have worked in cahoots with Alice and Patrick, but there was no reason for them to do so. Neither Alice nor Patrick had anything to gain from Roger's death, so why would they agree to commit murder in order to help Arthur out?

In short, Alice and Patrick had the means and the opportunity, but no motive. Arthur had a clear motive, but no means or opportunity. And there was no compulsion or reason for any of them to have worked together and combine means, motive and opportunity together.

The more she thought about it, the more it made her head hurt. Tomorrow they'd go and speak to Arthur. That would let them get a sense of what he was like, allow them to draw some more information out of him and — hopefully — start to make some progress in what was fast looking like an impossible case to crack.

33

With the dawn of a new day, Caroline felt physically better, but Operation Forelock had still left her head in a mess. It hadn't cleared by the time she got to the office, but she was alert enough to notice that Dexter's usual cheery enthusiasm seemed long gone.

'You alright, Dex?' she asked, sitting down next to him at his desk.

'Yeah. Yeah.'

'What's the matter?'

'Up all night, trying to work this out in my head. There's definitely something missing.'

'You mean on the historical side of things?'

'Yeah. You're right. It doesn't add up. We've got too much going on. Problem is, we're working backwards rather than starting with the evidence and going forwards.'

'We haven't got any evidence. Not really.'

'There's always evidence. We're making too many assumptions. We're jumping ahead. Let's look at pure facts.

The body was left on the rocks by Normanton Church. That's a fact. Anything more than that in terms of symbolism, motive — all guesswork. Hear me out. Blunt force trauma to the back of the head and strangulation. The strangulation says the killer was stronger than Roger Clifton, but the whack on the back of the head could've taken him down and given the killer enough of a head start to strangle him. Am I right in thinking there weren't any real signs of a struggle?'

'Apparently not.'

'So that tells me we're looking at someone potentially weaker than Roger who wasn't taking any chances. But they had to gain access through the gate, break the lock, then lift his body onto the rocks. Not strong enough to feel confident about beating him in a fight, but enough to lift his dead body and lay it out?'

'An accomplice. Alice Clifton kills him in a fit of rage. Patrick Walsh — big burly rugby player — does the heavy lifting, so to speak.'

'Again, that's a theory. No evidence at all. But — and forgive me for my own theory here — what if we're looking at it the wrong way? What if the head trauma and strangulation were because the killer wanted to make damn sure Roger was dead? Not a fight gone wrong or a cover-up, but planned in advance with a belt and braces approach.'

'You're still looking at one person lifting a dead body out of a car boot and over the ledge before laying it out on the rocks. Either way, we've got to be looking at a killer and an accomplice, at the very least. It still makes Alice Clifton and Patrick Walsh our main suspects.'

'But that makes no sense either. Why not dispose of the body somewhere else? Why lay him out in the middle of the biggest tourist attraction in the area? Roger disappeared off travelling enough and was pretty reclusive otherwise. They could've bumped him off, hidden the body and claimed ignorance. Everyone'd think he'd gone off on a jolly or disappeared. But instead they laid him out on full display, knowing damn well the estranged wife and her burly bit on the side would be prime suspects. Unless, of course, that was someone *else's* intention.'

'You mean someone framed Alice and Patrick?'

'Well, put it this way. I can't see them having pointed a massive arrow at themselves.'

'That's the thing, though. It's almost too massive. As if it could be a double bluff.'

'Theory again. And no real motive. Alice didn't need Roger out of the way. Sure, he was an arsehole, but he wasn't a problem for her. She had the house, they barely saw each other, she had no financial interest in the business. Far too much of a risk to kill Roger for virtually no gain.'

'But that's the problem. No-one had anything to gain from killing Roger. Other than the brother, I mean, but he wasn't even in the country at the time.'

'Yeah. I dunno. I still think we're missing something historical. You're right on the symbolism, but I think we're looking in the wrong place. I think it's historical symbolism, not religious.'

'Is that based on theory or evidence?' Caroline asked with a wry smile.

'Copper's intuition,' Dexter joked.

'Good luck getting that to stand up in court. Can you narrow it down at all?'

Dexter pursed his lips and shook his head. 'Not really. But I agree with you on one thing: the killer chose the church for a reason.'

'Then we need to find out more about the location. See if we can pin down a reason why it might've been picked. Sooner or later, things will start to piece together. What was the name of that history geek? The one with the stupid jumpers.'

'Howard Smallwood?'

'That's the one. You still got his number?'

'Yeah. Reckon it's worth giving him a call?'

'Probably not, but if it stops you moping about and means you'll get on with stuff, it's got to be worth investing ten minutes. Come on, follow me.'

Caroline led Dexter through into her office and tapped the phone number Dexter gave her into her office landline, which she put on speakerphone. 'Over to you, Columbo.'

Dexter waited for the call to connect and Howard Smallwood to answer.

'Mr Smallwood? Dexter Antoine from Rutland Police. We met at Otters recently.'

'Ah, yes! I remember. How can I help? Have you caught your killer yet?'

'Almost. I was actually wondering if we might be able to pick your brains a little more.'

'I'm not sure you'll find much, but you're welcome to have a go. What can I do you for?'

'It's about Normanton Church. We think the killer

picked that site for a reason, and we think it might've had some historical significance of some sort. We were wondering if you knew of anything in the church's history which might have made it stand out, somehow.'

'Well, you know about the deconsecration and raising of the church floor, don't you?'

'Bits, yeah.'

'That was all as a result of the planned flooding. Without that, the church wouldn't be there now. It was a community effort that saved it and got the work done.'

'Do you know who organised it?'

Howard exhaled heavily. 'Not off the top of my head. I've got a copy of the petition in my archives somewhere. Might take me a few days to dig it out, but I can take a look. Mind you, I imagine everyone will be long gone by now. I was only a boy at the time, myself. Anyone who was an adult then will be in their seventies at the very least now.'

'If you could take a look, I'd really appreciate it.'

'Of course. Not a problem. Sorry I can't be of more help.'

'No, please don't apologise. You've been great. I'm just sorry we can't be more specific in what we're looking for.'

'Well, if anything else pops to mind, you've got my number. I'm going away next week, though — late Sunday, early hours of Monday — so if you need me after that I'll be incommunicado.'

'Don't worry, we hope to have everything sewn up before then,' Dexter said.

'I hope so. Shout if you need me!'

Caroline chuckled as Dexter ended the call. 'Mad as a box of frogs.'

'No madder than us bumbling about like a tit in a trance.'

'Well,' Caroline said, looking up at the clock on the wall, 'it's about time we headed off to see Arthur Clifton. The site'll be open by now. He's our only man with a motive, after all.'

They headed out, as planned, to meet Arthur Clifton at the construction company's offices — the company which now bore the same name as its owner. There was a different feel around the place compared to their last visit. When they'd come before, there was a sense of suspicion and unease, as if no-one quite knew what was going to happen. This time there was an air of stability, of things getting back to normal.

'Hello again,' Sonya Smith, the office manager, said as they pulled up in the yard. She was leaning against the wall of the hut, smoking a cigarette.

'Morning. How's it all going?' Caroline asked.

'Alright, I think. Looks like we've all still got jobs, so that's the main thing.'

'Good. Is Arthur in?'

'In there,' she said, nodding her head towards the building she was leaning against.

Caroline and Dexter stepped inside, to find an attractive, tanned man hunched over a laptop.

'Hi,' Caroline said, jolting him back to reality.

'Hi, can I help?'

'You're Arthur, are you?'

'Yeah, I am.'

'DI Caroline Hills. This is DS Dexter Antoine. We're leading the investigation into your brother's death. Have you got a few minutes? It'd be good if we could chat.'

'Well I can't see it being any more painful than trying to sort out these bloody spreadsheets. Right now I'd take waterboarding over this, so fire away.'

'Were you and Roger close?' Caroline asked, sitting down on a spare chair.

'Not massively, no. I don't know what you've already heard, but I've been living in Spain, so obviously we weren't physically close. If you mean the other sense, let's just say we were brought up by a traditional sort of father. A stiff handshake counted as intimacy.'

'So have you moved back to the UK now?'

'Uh, well I hope not. Obviously I came back when I heard about what happened to Roger and I found out he'd left the company to me. I'm spending a bit of time getting to grips with where it is, what's going on, then I'll probably put someone in charge of the day-to-day running of it.'

'Have you got a business background then?'

'Yeah, I've run a couple of bars and things over in Spain. Totally different kettle of fish to this, though. Construction never really interested me. One of the reasons why I went off and did my own thing instead of getting involved with the family business in the first place.'

'Someone mentioned to us that you and Roger drifted apart over the years. Would you say that's the case?'

Arthur shrugged. 'We lived in different countries. So compared to growing up in the same house, yeah, obviously we were further apart. We didn't have a falling out or anything like that, though. We were just never close.'

'Did you know Roger had left the company to you before he died?'

'No, no idea. First thing I heard was when Alice spoke to the solicitor to find out what she should do. Apparently he'd filed documents with them years ago.'

'And he never told you?'

'No. But then again we didn't really speak, so there wasn't the opportunity to.'

'How did Alice react when she found out?'

Arthur sighed and leaned back in his chair. 'I think she was probably expecting to inherit the company herself. She didn't seem too happy about it. Not at first, anyway.'

'How do you mean?'

'Oh, she was ranting and raving about it all and threw me out. I think she was just upset and coming to terms with what had happened to Roger. It's a lot to try and process.'

'Threw you out? You were in the house?'

Arthur shuffled awkwardly. 'Yeah. Yeah, I was staying there.'

'Since when?' Caroline didn't recall seeing any sign of Arthur when she'd visited the Clifton residence.

'Only a few days. Things are alright now, though. We sat down and had a chat yesterday and worked out a few potential options. Enough to keep her quiet for a bit, anyway.'

'Options? What options?'

'Oh, we spoke about potentially giving her a share, making her a director. Sorting something out. Like I say, just a bone to keep her happy and quiet for now. No idea what'll actually happen, if anything. I'll need to speak to the brief again and find out what my obligations are.'

'Presumably none if the company's all yours.'

'You'd think so.'

'So are you staying with Alice now?'

'No, I'm at a hotel in town.'

'Which one?'

'Does it matter?'

'Only if you think it's worth hiding from us.'

Arthur looked at them for a few moments before speaking. 'The Wisteria,' he said.

Caroline and Dexter left the meeting a little over half an hour later, feeling even more confused than before they'd gone in.

'I don't buy it,' Caroline said, starting up the car.

'How so?'

'Well, come on. Roger Clifton, who hasn't seen his brother in years, leaves his successful construction business to him, despite having no interest or experience in construction?'

'He's got business experience.'

'Yeah, running bars in Spain. And why didn't Alice Clifton mention that he was back in the country and had been staying with her?'

'It's a bit odd, but not suspicious in itself.'

'I dunno. We need to find out when Roger filed those documents leaving the company to Arthur. And we need to know for sure if Arthur knew about it. See what we can find out about his financial situation, too. If it turns out he knew he'd be left the company and was in financial shit of his own, we've got a perfect motive.'

'What, you think Arthur could be responsible?'

Caroline cocked her head and narrowed her eyes as she focused on the road in front. 'Who knows? Suspect everyone, Dex. Always a good general rule.'

Before she could put the car into gear, her phone started to ring. She answered it through the car.

'DI Hills.'

'Hi, it's Aidan. I've got something,' Aidan said. 'I've been onto the airlines, trying to find out when Arthur Clifton came back to the UK. He's been back in the country for three weeks.'

'Seriously?'

'Yep. He was here a whole week and a half before Roger died.'

'Shit. He told us he came back when he heard the news.'

'Then he lied. And that opens up the question of what else he's been lying about.'

Caroline closed her eyes and sighed. 'He's got no reason to lie otherwise. But why try and get away with it? He must know we can check passenger lists and get the evidence.'

'Yeah. It doesn't sound right.'

'Right. Well, we know he's been staying at the Wisteria, so we'll head over there and speak to them. Maybe they'll be able to confirm how long he's been there.'

'Good stuff, I'll let you know if I hear anything else.'

Caroline ended the call, then jumped at the sound of someone tapping on her window. She turned to see a man in a hi-vis vest, and rolled her window down.

'Hi. Sorry,' he said, noticing he'd made her jump. 'You the police?'

'Yes, DI Caroline Hills. This is DS Dexter Antoine. And you are…?'

'Uh, do I have to give my name?'

'Well, no. Why? What's up?'

'I just wanted to say I saw something which might be useful, that's all.'

'What sort of thing?'

'Well, heard it, mostly. Arthur was here a couple of weeks ago, back when Roger was still around. They were having this almighty barney in the office. I know I should'nt've, but I got a bit closer to see what it was all about, like. We'd never seen Arthur before and we didn't know who he was till he took over the company, but then it all made sense. They was arguing about money and stuff.'

'He was here? What day was this?'

'Couldn't tell you. But yeah, I remember hearing Arthur say he was out of money. "Totally fucked" was the words he used. He was telling Roger how he was entitled to a share in the company and all that. Then we heard someone coming, so we scarpered.'

'I'll need to get all this down in an official statement from you,' Caroline said.

'Oh. Uh, I dunno. I mean, I don't want to rock the boat or nothing…'

Caroline and Dexter shared a look. They knew where to find him if they needed him. She handed the man her card. 'Alright, well this is my number and my email address. If you think of anything else, get in touch, alright? You never know. It could be the key to catching whoever killed Roger.'

34

Caroline and Dexter drove back into Oakham, skirting the town centre to head to the Wisteria Hotel. They parked up in the hotel's car park, having stopped momentarily to let a fire engine with full sirens leave Oakham Fire Station, which was directly opposite.

Having manoeuvred her Volvo into a spot she was almost certain she wouldn't be able to get out of again, Caroline and Dexter got out of the car and headed for the hotel's reception desk, smiling and nodding at the doddery old gardener as they passed.

The woman on reception — Katie, according to her name badge — smiled as they entered and welcomed them.

'No reservation, I'm afraid,' Caroline said, showing Katie her badge. 'I'm Detective Inspector Caroline Hills, and this is Detective Sergeant Dexter Antoine. We're looking for some information about a guest who's been staying here.'

'Okay... Is there a problem at all?' Katie asked.

'We don't know yet. Do you have a man by the name of Arthur Clifton staying here?' Caroline could tell by the look on her face that they did, but she made a show of checking the system on her computer anyway.

'Yes, we do. I don't know if he's here at the moment, though. He tends to leave after breakfast and doesn't come back until late, from what I can tell.'

'It's fine,' Caroline said, smiling. 'We don't need to speak to him. Can you tell us how long he's been a guest here, please?'

'Well, on this particular stay it's only since Monday night, but he did have another stay with us very recently.'

'How recently?'

'He was with us for almost two weeks, then checked out for a few days, before coming back on Monday.'

'I see. Do you have dates for that first stay, please?' Caroline jotted down the dates that were on the screen, knowing she now had evidence that Arthur Clifton had been less than honest with them about his whereabouts. 'That's brilliant. Thank you. You've been more help than you can possibly know.'

Caroline and Dexter left the Wisteria a few minutes later with a spring in their steps, giving an even bigger smile to the doddery old gardener as they headed back to the car.

35

Arthur Clifton looked downtrodden but determined as he sat opposite Caroline and Dexter in the interview room. Caroline had ordered his arrest, now knowing he'd been in the country far longer than he'd admitted — and was in Rutland on the night his brother was murdered.

She'd decided against conventional interview technique, and was instead going for the jugular. They already knew Arthur had lied to them, and she wanted to catch him off-guard from the start.

'You told us you came back to the UK because you heard Roger had died. Is that right?' she asked.

'Yes.'

'So why were you seen at the yard, arguing with Roger, days before his death?'

The colour began to drop from Arthur's face. 'Well, I dunno. Someone must be mistaken.'

'Okay. So why does the Wisteria Hotel have a record of you being in the country and staying with them before

Roger died? In fact, you were here on the night he was murdered, weren't you?'

'Umm. Look, this isn't what it seems, I can promise you.'

'You might as well just tell us the truth, Arthur. It's much quicker and cheaper than me having to pick up the phone to UK Border Control.'

Arthur let out a huge sigh. 'Alright. Yes, I was here. But that still doesn't mean I did anything. Look, I didn't know I was going to inherit the company. I had no clue about that at all until the lawyer got in touch. I don't even want the bloody thing, anyway. What do I know about construction? That's not my game.'

'On that note, why did you come back to the UK?' Caroline asked.

Arthur closed his eyes. 'Because I'd run out of money. The bar business went tits up. I thought I could rely on my family for a bit. Thought they might at least be willing to help me out. But Roger pretty much told me to piss off. Said he had no intention of helping me out. That's what he was like.'

'But you're financially stable now you've got the company, aren't you?'

'Honestly? I don't know. Maybe, maybe not. But I swear, I had no idea I was even in line for it.'

'So why would Roger leave you the business but not want to lend you any money when things went sour for you in Spain?'

'I have no bloody idea. I wish I knew. The only thing I can think of is he was respecting the family's wishes. Grandad's wishes. He wouldn't have wanted the business to leave the family, and he definitely wouldn't want it going to a leech like Alice.'

'The leech whose house you chose to stay at?'

'Briefly. Like I say, I'm brassic. The hotel bill's going on what's left of my credit card, and even that's creaking.'

'I've got to say, Arthur, it's not quite adding up. Pardon the pun. Did you kill Roger in a fit of rage? You'd had to leave Spain when your business went to the wall, and your own brother wouldn't lend you a helping hand.'

'No. We argued, yes. But no, I didn't kill him.'

'Where were you on the night he died?' Caroline asked.

'Asleep. I was staying at the Wisteria, wasn't I? I was in bed.'

'From what time?'

Arthur sighed again. 'I dunno. But it was a Saturday night. I was in the bar in the evening. I ate there and stayed for a few drinks, then went up. Look, why don't you just check the CCTV? You'll see me in the bar. Check the cameras on the front door. You'll see exactly when I came in and exactly when I went back out again the next day. In fact, I'm pretty sure the next time I left was when I got the call to say he'd died. Check the cameras. You'll see it all there.'

Caroline was seething, but she didn't show it. If Arthur was telling the truth, this would be another dead-end. In any case, she still felt sure the Patrick Walsh avenue showed more promise. Alice Clifton had blown a gasket when she found out Arthur would inherit the company. She'd clearly at least half-expected to get it herself, so potentially had that motive. If no-one else knew Arthur was in line to inherit the company, how could he have known himself?

Her head pounding, she ended the interview and left the room, having decided there was only one option left. Arthur had to be bailed.

36

Once they got back to the incident room, Caroline took a few minutes to go through the evidence and information about Arthur Clifton with Aidan, then stepped out into the main incident room and briefed the rest of the team.

'Either way,' she said, 'we need to gather as much as we can here. We can't prove anything one way or another without more evidence. Aidan, get onto the Wisteria and pull the CCTV between Saturday evening and Sunday morning on the night Roger died. We need to track down his movements from when he came back into the country, too. We need CCTV from the airport. Find out if he gets into a cab, on a bus, train, whatever. From there, find out where he went. Trace his movements. Sara, I need you to get hold of the solicitor who's been handling Roger's business affairs. Find out for certain when Arthur first knew he was being left the company. If it's before Roger died, we could be home and dry.'

'Do you think it's him?' Sara asked.

'Honestly? I don't know. If it is, why the religious symbolism? Why go to all the effort of taking the body down to Normanton and placing it on the rocks?'

'Diversion tactic? To be fair, it's worked. We've spent a week and a half assuming it's connected with religion somehow. What if it was all a massive red herring?'

'Then why not use a more accessible church? Normanton's got to be one of the most difficult-to-access churches in the country.'

'Exactly. It looks like it's been chosen specifically, and we're running around like headless chickens trying to find out why. What if it wasn't? Or what if it was, but purely for the purposes of throwing us off track?'

Caroline stopped for a moment. She had to concede that it was, of course, possible. But something still didn't sit right. The religious aspect wasn't a hill she was prepared to die on, but she felt sure it fitted into the equation somewhere, somehow.

'What if it's all linked?' Dexter said. 'What if there's a connection between the church, the history of the area and Arthur coming back to the UK a week and a half before his brother's murder?'

'Such as?'

'I don't know. But it's all too weird otherwise.'

'It's weird whichever way we look at it, Dex. Nothing about this case is normal. Have we had the library CCTV back from the council yet?'

'Not yet, no,' Sara said, looking a little embarrassed. 'I've been on at them again this morning, but they're dragging their heels.'

'For Christ's sake, we asked for it two days ago. Get onto them again. Put a rocket up their arse. Tell them if it's not here within the next few hours, we'll get a court order.'

'Will do.'

'In the meantime, my brain is at severe risk of actually melting if I don't take half an hour, so I'm going for a walk. Anyone need anything from town?' Caroline was pleased to see heads shaking rather than shopping lists being thrust at her, and smiled inwardly as she looked forward to a break in the fresh air.

A few minutes later she was strolling down Church Street, the warm sun on her face, a gentle breeze in her hair and the stunning Church of All Saints looming over her to the left. She couldn't deny Oakham was a beautiful town to walk round, and she told herself she'd make much more of an effort to do this — daily, if possible — and not only when she'd come so close to a complete breakdown that she needed the air and the space. Mark was right. It'd be good for her.

A little further down the road, she noticed an A-board outside Costa Coffee advertising the new Orbis restaurant and bar, reachable by a small passageway next to the coffee shop. She'd heard good things, and made a mental note to check it out. A moment or two after she'd walked past the sign, she stopped herself. No, she wasn't going to make a mental note. She and Mark needed a night out together. She decided to bite the bullet and book a table for later that week.

As she rounded the corner into the passageway, she noticed a couple standing a few feet short of the restaurant, locked in an embrace. It took a second or two before it registered, but once it had, she stepped back just as quickly as she'd gone forward. Edging herself slowly around the wall again to confirm her suspicions — and steadying her mobile phone to snap a couple of pictures — she tensed her jaw as she felt Operation Forelock move one step closer to closure. There was no mistaking it. The kissing couple were Alice Clifton and Patrick Walsh.

37

Back in the incident room, Caroline felt more energised and invigorated than she had in a long time. She now felt more certain than ever that Patrick Walsh was the key to unlocking what had happened to Roger Clifton. Until now, rumours of his affair with Roger's wife had been just that — rumours. The Cliftons' daughter had seemed a reliable enough witness, but now Caroline had incontrovertible proof that something was going on.

She now felt sure they had enough to arrest and begin questioning Patrick Walsh, but she didn't want to dive in. As things stood, all their evidence was circumstantial. The moment Walsh was booked into the custody suite, the clock would start ticking and they'd be given twenty-four hours to either convince the Crown Prosecution Service to authorise a murder charge, or they'd have to release him. Caroline wanted to get all her ducks in a row before they did that. She wanted to make sure there was no way the slimy Patrick Walsh could wriggle out of it. Once he was in, she wanted to be sure he wasn't getting out again. She needed to place him at the crime scene, or at the very least get hold of that CCTV evidence from the library which could go some way to proving Walsh sent Roger Clifton the emailed death threat.

Dexter knocked gently on her office door before letting himself in.

'I didn't want to say anything in front of the others, but I've been doing a bit more research and I think I might have something that could be useful,' he said.

'Go on.'

'Well, I like to try and keep my ear to the ground. Not usually much call for it round here, but you never know, right? Anyway, I did a bit of digging and I found a Facebook group about local history stuff. One guy on there posted quite a lot of photos of the Hambletons and the area before Rutland Water was built. The way he was talking, he seemed quite nostalgic about it all. Seemed pretty negative about what had happened in the sixties and seventies. Anyway, I sent him a message saying I was new to the area, interested in history and all that, and—'

'You sent him a message?'

'Yeah. Not as me, though. I've got a few dummy Facebook accounts in different names I use for stuff like this. Just in case, you see. As far as he knows, my name's Nick Connor.'

'Nick Connor?'

'Character from a book I read. Wasn't very good, but the name stuck with me. Anyway, we started chatting and I sort of played along, pretended I didn't know the history but was shocked and thought it must have been horrendous for the families that lived there, all that sort of thing. At that point he started coming out of his shell.'

'And what's this guy's name?'

'Edward Picton. I don't think that's his real name, though. Apparently he's got six Facebook friends and no pictures of himself. Couldn't find a record of anyone living locally with that name, either, even though he claims to live in Rutland. Anyway, we carried on talking and I made it sound like I was on his side with everything, and before I know it he's mentioned a private, hidden Facebook group he's a member of. Apparently there's a small handful of people who've never been able to let go of the past and who are still fighting the cause of the displaced families.'

'Fifty years later?'

'Exactly. It's all very underground, if you'll pardon the pun. I didn't really get a proper sense of what its purpose was or whether or not they had an aim. Just seems to be a load of bitter old people whinging about the way things used to be. But the point is it just goes to show there are still people who think that way. It's entirely possible the historical aspect might be a motive here. I'm looking into the members at the moment. I'll see if any of them are using real names or if we can track down who they are. Could at least be names we can add to our list and see if they pop up on the library CCTV or appear anywhere else in the investigation.'

'Only in your spare time, alright? We're a small team, Dex. We need to stay focused. You've got to keep your head in the game here and work on the lines of inquiry we've already got open. We can't have too many different leads or we'll lose focus and the right one'll be gone.'

'Gotcha. Mum's the word.'

'Thanks, Dex. Oh, by the way, I'll be late in tomorrow. Got an appointment first thing. Can you keep an eye on things and get the ball rolling for a court order for the library CCTV? We'll need to move on that quickly if nothing comes in by the end of the day.'

'Acting Detective Inspector Antoine. Got a nice ring to it.'

Caroline laughed. 'Yeah. Well don't get too attached to it, will you?'

38

The next morning, Caroline pulled her car into the now-familiar car park and turned off the engine. It wasn't a place she enjoyed visiting, but she hoped today could signal that it wouldn't be necessary to make too many more visits.

She walked over to the pay and display machine, bought a ticket and put it on her dashboard, before locking her car and walking into the main building.

A little over twenty minutes later, she was sitting in a comfortable chair inside the brightly-lit consulting room of Mr Pankash Anand, the man who'd come to know her more intimately than her own husband over recent months.

'How have you been getting on?' he asked her, his kind face and gentle smile immediately putting her at ease, as it always did.

'Okay, I think.'

'Any side effects? Dizziness? Vomiting?'

Caroline shook her head. 'No, nothing like that. I've been fine.'

'Alright, good. Well, as you know, we did some scans last week to try and get a better idea of how things are progressing and to see where we go from here. The upshot of it is that there has been some progress, but not quite as much as we'd like. We've seen some shrinkage of the tumour, but it really is pretty minimal. To be honest, if we continued with the treatment as is, at best I'd predict little to no change over the coming months, with the distinct possibility that it could potentially grow or spread further, which of course is what we want to avoid.'

Caroline swallowed. 'Right. What does that mean?'

'Well, there's no real way of knowing what damage the cancer could be doing to your ovaries in the long run. But, to be honest, the same could be said of the treatment. As things stand it's been quite targeted. We'd hoped the paraplatin on its own would be enough, but I think now we need to think longer term. There are two potential routes here. We could look at a more generalised chemotherapy, which of course has its own worries and side effects. We'd be talking hair loss, more extreme nausea, exhaustion. Chemotherapy attacks all fast-growing cells, even the healthy ones. The other option, and if we go down this route we'll need to move fast, is the surgical option. In my opinion, the tumour is small enough to operate on, but it's marginal. We'd need to operate quickly, because if it were to grow any more, we'd need to go down the heavy chemotherapy route anyway to shrink the tumour enough to get it to an operable state again. Does that make sense?'

'Yeah. I think so. To be honest, I'm struggling with the exhaustion as it is. What would the surgical route mean?'

'It'd be an overnight stay, at the least. Antibiotics, potentially intravenous steroids.'

'Would I be left with a scar?'

'There would be a surgical scar, yes. We'd go in through the abdominal wall. But that route isn't risk-free, either. I have to tell you there is a chance we'd have to take out the uterus or Fallopian tubes if there's a chance the cancer has spread, or if it's deemed safest to do so.'

The thought sent shockwaves through Caroline. She and Mark had never intended to have more children, but the prospect of having the possibility taken away from her was heartbreaking. More than that, in that instant it made her feel less of a woman.

But there was no denying further, heavier chemotherapy wasn't an option either. She'd been fortunate with the paraplatin. As a targeted treatment, it meant she'd had no hair loss or outward physical signs of cancer. She'd had the usual vomiting and exhaustion — not that she'd admitted that to the consultant. Now, there was nowhere left to run. She either went down the intense chemotherapy route with all that entailed, or she opted for surgery and the scars she'd be left with for life — with that as the best possible outcome of that particular option.

She leaned back in her chair and contemplated what life was going to become. Either way, she had to face up to it. She was going to need to tell Mark. It would affect her work, her home life, her relationships. There was no way out of it. No way of hiding it. Not anymore.

39

Caroline headed into work, glad to be able to dive into something which would take her mind off the appointment she'd just had.

Almost as soon as she arrived, Sara Henshaw updated her on what she'd missed.

'Good news and bad news,' she said. 'CCTV came in from the library just after you left yesterday. I've gone through it all, but there's no-one of interest at all, at least not around the time the email was sent.'

'No Patrick Walsh?'

'No. No-one on our list of suspects. No-one I recognised at all. I asked the library for anyone who used the computer terminals within two hours of the time the email was sent, but no-one had. It was a pretty quiet day by all accounts. So either the person who sent it isn't the person who killed Roger, or they're someone we haven't met or spoken to yet.'

'Or they accessed the library's wifi from outside the building.'

'Or that. There's external CCTV on the corner of Burley Road, which covers the roundabout area. I don't think it's going to be much use, though.'

'So what are our options?'

Sara sighed. 'Difficult to say. I need to speak to the tech guys and see if there's a way it could've been done remotely. Leave it with me.'

Caroline thanked Sara, feeling once again as if they'd hit a brick wall. Every time there was the possibility of a lead or a breakthrough, it seemed as though something else pulled the rug from under their feet.

Barely a few seconds after Sara left, there was a knock at the door.

'Come in.'

'Got something for you,' Aidan said. 'Phone records for Patrick Walsh. Could potentially be good news, but there's a caveat.'

'Go on.'

'Okay. On the night Roger Clifton was murdered, Walsh definitely wasn't at home. Based on cell site data, if he had his phone on him, he wasn't even in Oakham. But coverage is patchy, so we can't pin him down exactly. There's actually a pretty wide area he could've been in — nearly ten kilometres across — but guess what's right near the centre of it?'

'Please tell me the answer is Normanton Church.'

Aidan passed her a sheet of A4 paper, on which a map was printed, showing the overlay of the cell site data. Every mobile phone constantly pings nearby cell towers to maintain a reception, and most are connected to multiple towers at once. Each tower doesn't know where that mobile phone is, but it does know its distance. By knowing a phone was a specific distance from multiple different masts, it was possible to narrow its location down to within a few feet in some areas of the country. In Rutland, however, where cell masts were few and far between, it was a very different matter.

'Jesus Christ. That's amazing, Aidan,' Caroline said, confirming her hopes that Normanton Church sat nicely in the middle of the area in which Patrick Walsh's phone was known to have been.

'It is, but it's nowhere near enough. There are a million and one other places inside that patch where he could've been. It still doesn't place him at Normanton.'

'It doesn't, but it's a bloody good start. It's another step closer, without a doubt.'

'Certainly doesn't take him out of the picture just yet.'

'It's more than that. This might even be enough to bring him in and start to pick holes in his story.'

'Perhaps. I'm not so sure. I think we need something more concrete before we bring him in. We don't want him wriggling off. And if it's not him, we're up shit creek without a paddle. The guy's virtually a celebrity.'

Although she could see the sense in what Aidan was saying, Caroline had been sure since the moment she set eyes on Patrick Walsh that he was her man. So far, nothing had dissuaded her from that notion. On the contrary, every time they unpicked another piece of information, it seemed to lead them one step closer to him. There was nothing conclusive, but to Caroline that was only a sign that Patrick

Walsh had covered his footprints well. To get any closer, they needed to put him in the spotlight, find the holes in his defence and pick it apart until he had no choice but to tell them what had happened.

'I hear what you're saying, Aidan, but I've made a decision. Arrest Walsh on suspicion of murder. Bring him in.'

40

Although there were many questions Caroline wanted to ask Patrick Walsh, some of them would have to wait.

The process of the formal police interview under caution was always much the same, regardless of the suspect. The first interview was designed to elicit the basic facts, regardless of what they already knew to be true. The idea was to give the suspect enough rope to hang themselves with. Even if they knew damn well where they'd been at the moment the crime was committed, it was far more advantageous to ask them where they were than to tell them. The second interview could then be used to reveal the evidence which would prove they'd lied in their first interview. At this point, the pressure would be applied in the hope of the suspect admitting the truth under the pressure of growing and overwhelming evidence.

She chose to conduct the interview herself, with Dexter sitting alongside her. Walsh had opted to attend the interview on his own, without a solicitor or legal representation. This was something many suspects did, presumably in an attempt to give the impression that they had nothing to hide. In reality, it did the complete opposite. An innocent person arrested for murder doesn't try to wriggle out of it on their own; they immediately call a solicitor and seek the best legal advice possible to clear their name. Walsh's approach smacked of arrogance, and Caroline didn't like it one bit.

Walsh sailed through the first interview, claiming he was at home at the time Roger Clifton was murdered — something they now knew to be untrue. He also claimed he had no intimate connection with Alice Clifton, and knew the family only through their involvement with Empingham Methodist Church. Caroline had seen with her own eyes that this was also a lie.

Having left him to stew for an hour or two before interviewing him the first time, Caroline was tickled when Walsh presumed he was then free to go. She'd taken great delight in disabusing him of that notion, telling him they'd need to interview him again later in the day, then escorting him back to his cell.

Although the clock wasn't strictly on their side, and they only had twenty-four hours from booking him in until they had to either charge or release him, Caroline was a fan of using it to her advantage. Winding the clock down meant Walsh would either get increasingly annoyed and frustrated or — perhaps even better — would gain a false sense of confidence, presuming the police were struggling. Knowing Walsh's arrogant personality, Caroline was willing to put money on the latter.

The team had been busy collating further evidence, looking for proof that he'd sent Roger Clifton the death threat by email, and were attempting to make forensic links. Walsh'd had his DNA taken on being booked into custody, and Caroline had been frantically awaiting results of a link. She knew it was unlikely they'd come back in time, but waiting had the added benefit of leaving him to stew in his cell for a little while longer.

By the time Walsh's second interview rolled around, it was approaching midnight. Chief Superintendent Derek Arnold had hung around until just past ten, keen to keep abreast of the situation. After all, murder didn't often visit Rutland. But even he had given in to the call of home, leaving only Caroline, Dexter, Sara and Aidan in the office.

Caroline and Dexter sat down in the interview room, trying to look more awake and alert than Walsh, who'd had nothing to do but sleep in his cell for the past few hours, and hoped their fixes of black coffee and Haribo Tangfastics would keep them going long enough. With Walsh's custody clock running out late the next morning, they could be in for a long ride yet.

'So, Patrick. You told us you were at home on the night Roger Clifton was murdered, is that right?'

'Yes,' Walsh said, a little less certain than he had sounded earlier.

'Okay. We've got mobile phone cell site data which shows the approximate area your phone was in at the time. Do you want to change your answer based on that?'

At this point, most suspects tended to try to wriggle out of it by claiming they'd lost their phone or had left it somewhere accidentally. Proof of their mobile phone's location wasn't the same as proof of their location.

Walsh swallowed and sat back in his chair, folding his arms. He glanced off to the side, as if trying to concoct a story in his head.

'No comment.'

It was another common belief that no-commenting one's way through an interview would somehow absolve them of guilt. On the contrary, when cases reached court, judges tended to look unfavourably on uncooperative defendants.

'Okay, let's try something else,' Caroline said. 'You told us in your first interview that you had no real connection or relationship with any of the Clifton family, and that you knew them only through the church. Do you want to change anything there?'

Walsh shook his head. 'No.'

'I'd like you to take a look at this photo.' Caroline passed Walsh a printout of the photo she'd taken of him and Alice Clifton outside Orbis. 'Do you recognise the people in this photo?'

Walsh's jaw tensed. 'No comment.'

'Is the male you?'

'No comment.'

'I think it looks quite a lot like you.'

'No comment.'

'In fact, I think it is you. Do you recognise the female?'

'No. No comment.'

'I hate to burst your bubble, Patrick, but that is a comment. Is the female Alice Clifton?' Walsh didn't answer.

'That's you and Alice Clifton, isn't it, Patrick? What are you both doing in this picture?' Although it was blindingly obvious what they were doing, Caroline was keen to lead him into answering, as opposed to putting everything in front of him at once. 'Are you and Alice Clifton in a relationship? How long has that relationship been going on? Did you kill Roger Clifton because you wanted to be with his wife?'

'No. I didn't kill Roger.'

This was the first time Patrick had explicitly denied his involvement in the murder. Caroline pushed harder.

'It looks to me a lot like you did. Here you are, captured on camera, kissing Alice Clifton. Your phone indicates you were in the vicinity of Normanton Church at the time her husband was murdered. It's not looking great, is it?'

'I wasn't in Normanton. I was in Empingham.'

There was silence in the interview room for a second or two. Caroline glanced down at the cell site map she'd been given, and sensed Dexter doing the same. It was true. The highlighted area showing the possible locations of Patrick's phone did include Empingham. Walsh knew they had cell site data, but he hadn't seen the map so would have had no way of knowing how wide the radius was. He had no way of knowing it included Empingham. It would have been one hell of a gamble on his part, so Caroline's assumption had to be that he was telling the truth.

'Empingham? Why's that?'

Walsh let out a huge sigh. 'I was with Alice.'

'Alice Clifton?'

'Yes.'

'What for?'

Walsh looked up and made eye contact with Caroline. 'What do you think?'

'I don't know. You tell me.'

'Put it this way: I stayed overnight.'

'With a friend you vaguely knew from church?' Walsh didn't answer. 'Or is there a bit more to it than that?'

'You know damn well there is.'

'I know nothing until you tell me, Patrick. And from where I'm sitting it seems like a very good idea for you to start telling me, because right now you're on the verge of being charged with the murder of Roger Clifton.'

He looked at Caroline again. 'I didn't kill Roger. End of.'

'No, it's not "end of". This is very much the beginning. If you want anything ended, you'll need to tell us everything.'

Walsh seemed to consider this for a moment. Then he answered.

'I'm saying nothing. I want a lawyer.'

41

Caroline left the interview room feeling more frustrated than ever. She was almost certain she'd been on the verge of getting a confession out of Patrick Walsh, but now that seemed a million miles away.

Part of her felt worried at having let the custody clock run down so far. They were now more than halfway through, and she'd been left in the position of trying to get hold of a duty solicitor at gone midnight. She privately wondered whether that had been Walsh's plan all along. But then why admit the affair? None of it made any sense to her. She was tired. Knackered. Very little was going to make sense when her mind was like this.

She wondered if she might be able to grab an hour's kip somewhere — in her office, perhaps. She didn't do well with naps. She tended to wake up rattier than before, but it was the only option she had. There was no way she was going to get home before lunchtime. There was always a good chance, too, the custody clock could be extended if her superiors agreed a little more time was needed. It was an option that was only available in the most serious of cases, and there weren't many more serious than murder.

Caroline made her way back to the incident room, ready to update Sara and Aidan on their progress — or lack thereof — in Walsh's second interview. But before she could do so, the door flew open and Sara bundled out into the corridor.

'Oh! There you are. I was just coming down to find you.'

'Yeah yeah, alright,' Caroline said. 'I told you we'd be up when we were finished.'

'No, I wasn't chasing. I was coming to give you an update. There's been a development. A massive one.'

'What is it?' Caroline asked, narrowing her eyebrows as she felt the dull thud of exhaustion in her temples.

'It's Arthur Clifton — Roger's brother.'

'What about him, Sara? Spit it out.'

'He's been murdered.'

Sara's words hit Caroline like an icy bolt.

'What? How? Tell me,' she said, ushering Sara back into the incident room.

'We've got first responders on the scene at the moment, but from what we can gather so far, Arthur was walking up the driveway to Alice Clifton's house in Empingham when he was attacked. Too early to get too much detail, but it looks like a heavy blow to the back of the head, plus strangulation. Again.'

'Jesus Christ.' Caroline sat down in the nearest chair and tried to gather her thoughts. 'When?'

'Literally within the last hour. Alice Clifton heard something outside and went to look out the window. She says she saw someone running away, but it was so dark she couldn't make out anything else.'

'What the hell was Arthur doing there at that time of night?'

'No idea. But apparently he stinks of alcohol. Either

way, if we're assuming his and his brother's murders are linked, it can't have been Patrick Walsh. We've had him in custody since before lunch.'

'I know, Sara. I know. Jesus. I need a minute. Sorry.'

'It's fine, don't worry. I think we can safely say the killer's getting desperate, though. Look at what happened with Roger. That must've been planned meticulously. With Arthur, it's a case of jumping him in the dead of night while he's a few beers down, then scarpering. Whoever it is, they're panicking.'

'Or they desperately needed Arthur Clifton dead there and then.'

'In which case, we need to find out why.'

'Have you spoken to Chief Superintendent Arnold?'

'Not yet, no. I thought you should be the first to know.'

'Alright. Dexter's still downstairs. Let him know what you know. I'll call Arnold.'

Caroline waited for Sara to disappear out of sight, then she grabbed her keys and headed down to the car park. On her way, she called Derek Arnold. He picked up his phone just as she got to her car and sat inside.

'Caroline. How'd it go?' Arnold said.

'The interview? Not amazing. He shut down and started no-commenting, then demanded representation. Aidan's trying to get hold of an on-duty brief. Listen, something's happened. We've just had a call. There's been another murder.'

Arnold was silent for far longer than Caroline would've liked before speaking. 'Who?'

'Arthur Clifton,' Caroline said, almost whispering.

'The brother?'

'Yeah. The brother.'

'What happened?'

'Same MO.'

'I see.'

'That's all we know right now. I'm heading over to the scene now to see what I can—'

'No,' Arnold said, interrupting her.

'Sorry, sir?'

'No. No, you're not. Go home, Caroline. Get some sleep. We'll speak in the morning.'

Something in his tone of voice didn't quite sound right to her. 'Sir, I'm fine. Is something the matter?'

'I think it'd be better to talk about this in the morning, once we've both had some sleep.'

'I'd rather talk about it now, if that's okay.'

She heard Arnold sigh heavily at the other end of the phone. 'Alright. Go home, get some sleep, and don't come into the office tomorrow morning. I'm putting you on leave. We're handing the case over to EMSOU.'

'What? Why?'

'Why? You're not actually asking me that, are you? As if our previous chats weren't enough, you've let the case completely run away with you. It's now a double murder. And who knows how many more people he's got in his sights? You've got a former bloody international rugby player in custody for a murder he didn't commit and, quite frankly, you're causing far more trouble than you're solving right now. Listen, I know it's not necessarily your fault. I can tell something isn't right. Christ knows what it is, but either way you need to get home and rest, for both our sakes. I'll clear up the mess, I'll get EMSOU on board and with any luck we'll catch the person responsible sooner rather than later.'

There was a finality in Derek Arnold's tone that told her there was very little point in objecting. He'd made his decision, and that was that.

Consumed by rage, anger, heartbreak and regret, she let out an ear-piercing scream at the top of her lungs; a scream that reverberated around the interior of her car, ringing in her ears for seconds after she'd finished. But it had been a long time coming.

She opened her car door and stepped out onto the tarmac, feeling the cool night air and the gentle breeze on her face. She was lost and utterly alone.

'Oh, hey.' Dexter walked towards her. 'Sara just gave me the lowdown on what happened to Arthur Clifton. Fuck.'

'Yeah. Fuck.'

'You okay?'

'No. No, Dex, I'm not.'

'What's the matter?' Dexter said, letting her put her head on his shoulder.

'I'm off the case.'

'What do you mean?'

'I spoke to Arnold. He wants to hand control over to EMSOU. He wants me to take some time off.'

'Are you serious?'

'He is.'

'Oh, man. I'm sorry.'

'Don't be. What are you doing out here, anyway?'

Dexter clenched his jaw. 'I'm gonna head over to Empingham. See what we can get.'

Caroline nodded and closed her eyes.

'I mean, I can stay here. I don't need to go, I suppose. I probably shouldn't, actually. Wouldn't be very... Well, y'know.'

'Loyal?'

'I guess.'

'Don't worry about loyalty, Dex. Your only loyalty is to the victims and their families.'

'Alright. If you're sure.'

Caroline forced a smile. She'd felt certain he would stick by her and fight her corner. She didn't know why it always seemed to happen, but she found herself once again feeling betrayed and alone.

43

When Caroline finally got home, she slept until midday. Her first thought on waking was to call the office and get an update on Patrick Walsh, but she didn't. She knew what would have happened. His custody clock had run down, the murder of Arthur Clifton would mean he'd be heavily downgraded as a suspect in Roger's murder, and he'd have been released. But a nagging doubt stuck at the back of Caroline's mind.

What if this was all part of the plan? What if Patrick Walsh *had* killed Roger Clifton, and the reason Arthur was attacked and murdered so suddenly and desperately was because it *needed* to be done then? To her, it made perfect sense. If Arthur Clifton was murdered while Patrick Walsh was in police custody, that'd throw huge doubt on his guilt — as it had done already. Either way, there was nothing she could do. She was off the case.

Her phone vibrated on the bedside table beside her. She recognised the number immediately. It was the hospital. She pressed the volume button on the side of the phone to silence the call, and put it back down. She didn't care what they had to say. It was only going to be bad news. Good things weren't coming her way.

It took another half an hour for her to finally get up and go downstairs. She wanted to wait until she'd heard Mark go out to pick up the shopping, as he did every week. That way, she could ease herself into the day a little more easily.

She looked at the kitchen clock. Should she be having breakfast or lunch? It didn't seem to matter much either way. She took a bowl from the cupboard and put it on the kitchen work surface. As the porcelain touched the veneered wood, her eyes were drawn to a bottle on the side — one which had been there for a week or so and had largely become part of the furniture. She looked at it for a moment, admiring the way the clear liquid sat almost perfectly level with the top of the label. Before even thinking, she grabbed the bottle, unscrewed the cap and brought it to her lips, gulping down the bitter, aromatic gin. Stopping for breath, she put the bottle back down, feeling the rush of the alcohol almost immediately. The liquid settled, and it became clear how much she'd drunk. She looked behind her again, then took the bottle over to the sink and carefully added cold water until the original level had been restored.

She felt sick. Physically and mentally. She didn't know how she'd got here, nor did she care. She wanted out of it. She felt her phone vibrating in her pocket, and looked at the screen. The hospital again. She looked back at the bowl, still sitting in the place she'd left it, quietly waiting to see what food it would be paired with today. She was sure she'd never admired a piece of ceramic in quite this way before, but the fact of the matter was bowls just got on with it. They didn't worry about thoughts and feelings. They were never betrayed — other than in favour of another bowl, but she very much doubted that ever worried them.

She jumped at the loud click and rumble of Mark sliding open the patio doors. 'Morning. Or afternoon, should I say. How'd it all go?'

'You don't want to know.'

'No luck?'

'To say the least.'

'Wasn't it him?'

'I don't know.'

'Has he been released then?'

'Yes. I think so. Look, do we have to talk about this now?'

Mark looked wounded. 'No. I guess not. I just wanted to check you're okay, that's all.'

'I'm fine. I just want five minutes' peace. Is that too much to ask?'

Mark raised his hands in mock surrender and headed out into the garden. In that moment, Caroline felt closer than she ever had to crumbling completely.

44

The rest of the day had passed in a blur. Once mid-afternoon came around, Caroline had innocently suggested they fire up the barbecue and share a bottle of wine. The sharing aspect hadn't quite worked, and she'd drunk most of it herself. That had, naturally, led on to cider and beer, before spirits in the evening. Mark had mostly abstained, choosing instead to quietly berate her for drinking too much. But she really didn't care. She'd enjoyed the calm sense of relief the alcohol gave her. The next morning, though, her head was feeling something very different indeed.

She was woken by the sound of jangling keys. It was a sound she recognised, but not one she'd expected to be woken by. She rolled over and opened one eye, watching as Mark took the keys from the bedroom dresser and put them in his jacket pocket.

'Mark? What's going on?'

'It's alright. Go back to sleep. I left you a note downstairs.'

'A note? What for? What's going on?'

Mark sighed. 'I'm taking the boys to see Mum.'

'What? Without me?'

'She hasn't seen them in ages,' he said, ignoring her question. 'It'll do us all some good.'

'Mark, what are you saying? Are you planning on staying there?'

Mark sat down on the edge of the bed and looked at her. 'Caz, I can't stand to see you like this. The kids have picked up on it, too. They're scared and worried. I've asked you so many times what the problem is. I've tried to talk to you, I've tried guessing what's wrong, I've tried... I've tried, Caz. If you won't let me in and won't talk to me, what can I do? I can't help you if you won't let me help you.'

'I'm not asking you to help me.'

'I know. That's the problem. Look, I'll call you later on, alright? We'll only be there a couple of nights. Monday's a bank holiday anyway, so we can come back late in the evening if everything's alright. We'll play it by ear.'

'Play it by ear? Mark, Jesus Christ, give me a chance to wake up and process this. Are you leaving me?'

'It's just a couple of nights. The boys want to see their Grandma.'

Caroline sensed movement at the bedroom door. She sat up and felt the pounding of yesterday's alcohol in her head as she looked over towards them.

'Come and say goodbye, boys. We'll ring Mum when we get there, yeah?'

'Bye, Mum,' Josh said, giving her a cursory kiss on the cheek. He was growing old before his time. Archie came over and hugged her, showing a little more affection, but she could still tell he'd spotted something in her. Something that wasn't quite right.

'Just a couple of nights,' Mark said, almost whispering.

She looked at the boys and felt as though she'd lost them. She could see from the looks in their eyes that they barely knew her anymore.

By the end of the day, the house had never looked so clean. The only way she'd found to distract herself and her mind was to listen to the radio and clean the house from top to bottom. She'd vacuumed every room twice after discovering a new setting on the hoover that she'd never found before. Then again, she estimated she'd probably only used the thing twice in her life. Today was different. Today was about distraction. Purging the dirt. Keeping bad thoughts at bay.

One room'd had less attention than the others, though. She'd tried to avoid the kitchen where possible, not wanting to see the temptation of the alcohol bottles. She desperately wanted to just curl up in a ball with a large glass and drink herself to sleep, but there was still a part of her — a part she was grasping onto for dear life — that knew that wouldn't do any good.

She needed to keep things together as much as possible. She couldn't afford to spiral in on herself. She'd already lost the case, the respect of her colleagues and — only temporarily, she hoped — her family. If she couldn't keep control of her head, she'd lose everything else, too.

By the time the evening rolled around, her legs felt like lead. Her mental anxiety had provided far more nervous energy than her body had provided physical energy, and by now the latter was severely lagging. She collapsed onto the sofa, hoping she'd either regain some energy or drift off to sleep, before waking up and doing it all again. She only needed to distract herself until Mark and the boys were back. That'd be enough to ground her, focus her on what she needed to do.

She needed to tell Mark about the cancer. She knew that. But how could she tell him now? It'd either look like a cynical stunt to get him to come back, or he'd realise just how long she'd kept it to herself and would be devastated at the thought that she couldn't tell him about it.

She'd been fortunate, in a way. The cancer was ovarian, which gave very few noticeable symptoms. There was certainly nothing Mark would have spotted. The treatment, too, had been something she'd been able to hide. When she'd got the diagnosis, she was stunned. They were on the verge of leaving London for a better life. They were putting their troubles behind them. The last thing she wanted was to rock the boat, upset her family and put her brand new job in jeopardy. And when she was given the details of the proposed treatment plan — a course of paraplatin chemotherapy which would be unlikely to lead to hair loss or any noticeable side effects other than tiredness and nausea — she'd honestly believed she could get through it on her own. There had always been a decent chance of surgery being required once the chemotherapy had shrunk the tumour, but she'd told herself she'd cross that bridge when she came to it.

It had started as a matter of necessity. She'd tell Mark in a few days, she thought. Then days had become weeks, weeks became months and she'd realised there was no way she could sit him down and tell him what she'd hidden from him for so long. In any case, that would only be the tip of the iceberg.

There was a reason she didn't open up. It wouldn't be as simple as that. It was more a case of opening the floodgates.

She was jolted from her reverie by the sound of her phone. It was a different ring from normal. She looked at the screen. It was a FaceTime call from Josh. She accepted the call.

'Hey, you,' she said, trying to look as calm and happy as she could. 'How are you? How's Grandma?'

'Yeah, she's good. We're good.'

'Okay. Good. You having fun down there?'

'Not really. You know what it's like.'

Caroline let out a small laugh. 'Yeah, I do. Is this you telling me you've become a bona fide country bumpkin now, then?'

'Something like that, yeah. As long as I get a tractor out of it.'

'I'll see what we can do.'

Caroline saw Mark enter the room behind Josh, and in that moment she realised her son had called her on his own impulse, and not because he'd been told to.

'Hey,' Mark said, looking at the screen.

'Hi. You okay?'

'Yeah, no real change. We went out into town for a bit earlier, but I think the boys'd had enough. Mum's doing dinner.'

'At this time?'

'Was meant to be ready for five. You know what she's like. I told the boys to expect it around half eight.'

Caroline laughed again. Seeing Mark and Josh's faces had been a tonic for her. 'Where's Archie?'

'He's "helping" Mum,' Mark said, complete with air quotes.

'Ah. Half eight might've been optimistic then.'

Mark flicked his eyebrows up knowingly. 'We've shared a pack of Jaffa Cakes. We'll last. How are you doing? Getting some rest?'

'Sort of. I'm alright. I'm good.'

Mark nodded slowly. 'Good. I'm glad to hear it. Josh, go downstairs and see if you can speed things up with dinner, will you? I'm starting to get hungry here.' Josh did as he was told — not without the slight grunt of a boy fast becoming a teenager — and Caroline watched as he walked through the bedroom door and onto the landing. 'And really?' Mark asked.

'What do you mean?'

'How are you really?'

'I'm fine.'

'You don't look it.'

'Oh wow. Thanks.'

'Listen, we'll come back Monday night, okay? It gives you a couple of days to sort your head out. But please, look after yourself, yeah? Have some long baths. Candles. Nice music. Get takeaways. Indulge. You probably need it.'

The last thing she needed was private indulgence, but she was in no mood to argue with him. 'Yeah. I'll do my best.'

'Speak tomorrow, yeah?'

'Yeah.'

Caroline disconnected the call and put the phone down on the floor. Before she could organise her thoughts, there was a knock at the door.

She stood up and walked through into the hallway. She could tell from the blurred figure on the other side of the glass it was Dexter. She was sorely tempted to walk away and pretend she hadn't heard him knocking, but there was no way he was going to fall for that.

'What do you want, Dex?' she said, opening the door.

'Can I come in?'

'No.'

'Look, I know you're upset with me. I know you think I've been disloyal or whatever, but trust me, I haven't. The only reason I'm sticking with this is out of sheer loyalty to you.'

'And how do you figure that one out?'

'Because I'm doing it to prove us right and get to the bottom of things. Fuck EMSOU. I'm doing this for us.'

'Doing what?' She looked down at the cardboard box between Dexter's feet.

'Look, you might want to let me in. I think I know what's going on with the Clifton murders.'

46

Dexter emptied the box onto the coffee table in the living room as Caroline tried to get her head around what she was seeing.

'Dex, these are confidential documents. I'm off the case. I'm suspended. I'm not allowed to see these.'

'They're not the originals.'

'What, so you photocopied them to hide the fact you were breaking the law? That's even worse.'

'It's not breaking the law. It's circumventing procedure.'

As if her brain wasn't confused and muddled enough as it was, Caroline was struggling to work out why Dexter was helping her now. If he'd wanted to do the right thing, why hadn't he fought her corner? He'd had his chance to display his loyalty and he'd chosen not to. And now here he was, risking his career in order to prove a point.

'Listen, I've been doing more research and digging.'

'Is this a history thing?'

'History is everything. Trust me on this. I've been

looking into everything that happened when Rutland Water was formed. The flooding of the villages, the compulsory purchase of the land, the petitions and protests at the time. I've been living and breathing this to the point where I can't see straight. The others think I'm mad. They're not having any of it. EMSOU don't even want to see my notes. But I really think I've got something.'

'Go on.'

'Alright. Here's a list of the companies that worked on the construction. There's colour coding to show which aspects they worked on. Some of them were involved in the demolition, some in the building of the dam, various things right up until the original project was deemed completed and signed off.'

'Right. And?'

'Notice any familiar names?'

Caroline scanned her eyes down the list. 'Well yeah, Arthur Clifton Construction. But what's that got to do with anything? They're the biggest local construction company, and they've been going for decades. Hardly surprising they were involved.'

'And what if I told you that every single other one of these companies no longer exists? They've all gone out of business or been sold off, closed down. Arthur Clifton Construction worked on the demolition and groundworks. They were involved in taking down people's houses and preparing the ground for the flooding. And they're the only company left. Anyone with a grudge would only have one company to target. One family. Roger Clifton, owner of the company? Murdered. The company passes down to his brother, who mysteriously appears back from Spain? Murdered. There's enough here to make a link, I'm sure of it, but we're missing something.'

'A suspect?'

Dexter nodded. 'Yeah. The biggest part of all.'

47

'So what do we know?' Dexter said, spreading a number of sheets of paper out over the table. 'We know there are people who're angry at what's happened in Rutland over the years. There's that Edward Picton guy who's still going on about the flooding of the villages. I wouldn't be surprised if he was our man, or if at the very least he could lead us to him. I'm still doing my best on that front, but I need to earn his trust. The fact that we can tie Arthur Clifton Construction in so heavily on this has got to be key. Roger and Arthur weren't killed because they were brothers; they were killed because they were the owner of the only existing construction company involved.'

'Okay, but let's roll back. Why now? Why wait until there's only one left?'

'Maybe they didn't.'

'No. Makes no sense. These have to be the first murders. They were so blatant and obvious. Roger Clifton was laid out on the rocks and his brother was bludgeoned and strangled on his own sister-in-law's driveway. It's got to be a grudge against their company specifically. Shit. What about the original Arthur Clifton? How'd he die?'

'I already checked it out. Meningococcal septicaemia and pneumonia. Not murder, if that's what you're getting at.'

'So Roger and his brother are the first generation that's been targeted, despite only being boys themselves when this all happened. How can we be so sure the link is with the creation of Rutland Water? It could be any business deal gone wrong, far more recently. There are plenty of people with grudges against construction companies.'

'Then why Normanton Church? I agree with you. The timing's weird. But there's got to be a reason for that. We just need to work out what.'

'If you're right, we need to set up a meeting with this Edward Picton. Earn his trust. Arrange to meet him somewhere. As soon as possible. Who's due to inherit Arthur Clifton Construction now?'

'Yeah, Sara thought of that already.'

'I bet she did.'

'Situation unclear. In the hands of the lawyers.'

'Right. This isn't something I'd normally say, but tell them to slow the hell down. As soon as they determine someone as the rightful heir, that person's a sitting duck. We can't afford a third death on our hands. Not if we're as close as we think we might be.'

'On it. Shall I take these papers and things back with

me, then? Seeing as you don't want to break any rules or regulations.'

Caroline raised the corner of her mouth at Dexter's subtext. 'Y'know what, if you did accidentally leave them here I don't suppose it'd be the biggest problem in the world.'

48

Shortly after Dexter left that evening, Caroline went to bed. She woke up late the next morning, having slept more soundly than she had in a long time. She had no idea why, but it felt like something within her had settled.

She spent Sunday afternoon looking through the research and history notes Dexter had left on the coffee table. She'd made good use of the Companies House website, double-checking none of the other businesses existed anymore — not that she doubted Dexter's thoroughness — and made notes of the names of their directors. But no names stood out. Nothing seemed to tie in with anything they already knew.

Dexter, on the other hand, had been more than busy. In a matter of hours he'd managed to move things on with Edward Picton and had arranged a rendezvous for that evening. Dexter, under his alter ego, had claimed to be a descendant of one of the families who'd lived in the Hambletons before the flooding. Fortunately, he'd had the foresight to get hold of a list of those families — another document Caroline was yet to get round to — on the off-chance Picton managed to rumble him on that front. As far as Edward Picton was concerned, Dexter's alter-ego Nick Connor was a descendant of the Locke family, who'd lived in Middle Hambleton.

They'd arranged to meet at the Wheatsheaf in Greetham. Caroline had, of course, taken the opportunity to point out that this backed up her theory that every other pub in Rutland was called the Wheatsheaf. Neither of them knew what Edward Picton looked like, but he'd told Dexter's alter-ego Nick he'd turn up in a blue Ford Focus and would be wearing a black shirt and jeans. They'd arrived early, having planned to park up and wait for his arrival. It would be advantageous for them to get a good look at Picton before moving in, especially as they were without the necessary backup. With everything being done very much off the record, they couldn't afford to take any personal risks.

Caroline looked at the clock on Dexter's dashboard. There were still twenty minutes to go until the meeting time. She wound her window down a little to let some fresh air in, and listened to the trickle of the stream that ran down the side of the car park and the pub's beer garden. It looked like a wonderful place to spend a sunny afternoon, and she made a mental note to come here with Mark and the boys — when they were back.

'Is it wrong that I'm nervous?' Dexter asked.

'I think there's plenty to be nervous about.'

'I don't even know what I'm going to say. I've got this

whole back story about how my nan had an affair with a bloke from Antigua. I've spent more time worrying about how I'm gonna explain the colour of my skin than I have trying to figure out what I want to ask him.'

'It'll come. Don't worry. The main thing is getting ID on who he is. Then it's a case of finding out who else he's in contact with and narrowing it down to a suspect.'

'Yeah. Yeah, I know. I just don't want to fuck it up.'

'You're not going to fuck it up.'

'I've always worried about letting people down.'

'You're not going to let anyone down.'

'Yeah. I know. But I always worry about it. I always feel that pressure, y'know? I feel like I've let my mum and dad down by not being a doctor. I feel like I'm not doing enough for work, as if I should be at it twenty-four hours, constantly going over stuff.'

'Alright. Firstly, you're not far off. You spend far more time working over stuff than anyone else I know. And secondly, this is real-life policing. It's not like the telly. It's just a job. You leave it at the door.'

'Yeah, but I don't, do I? I always want to do everything the best I can.'

'Yeah, well you're lucky you're able to get close. Try having kids and a husband running around. Plus... plus other stuff. You're lucky you *can* do your best.'

'I just don't feel like I do, you know? I feel like I always come up short.'

'You're doing fine, Dex. More than fine. You have nothing to worry about. Trust me.'

'That's really kind and all that, but I dunno. I just feel like I have to—'

'Dex, I've got cancer.'

In that moment, all sound stopped. The air no longer whistled past the window. The stream no longer trickled behind them. She'd waited so long to say those words, rolling them over her tongue for weeks and months, and now they were out. And they hung in the air with an atmosphere heavier than she'd ever expected.

49

'How long?' Dexter said, finally breaking the silence.

'What, how long have I had it or how long have I got left?'

'How long have you had it. Dick.'

Caroline laughed. In one word, Dexter had both settled the atmosphere and cemented their friendship. 'It was diagnosed a week before we moved up here. Stage two, so you're not getting rid of me just yet.'

'What… I mean, where…'

'Ovarian. The lady bits.'

'I know what ovaries are. In a parallel universe I'm a doctor, don't forget.' Dexter was silent for a moment. 'That's ages. Why didn't you say anything?'

'I didn't think you were interested in my ovaries.'

'I'm not, but I'm interested in you being okay.'

'I'm fine.'

'You're not fine, you've got… You're not well.'

'It's okay, Dex, you can say it. It's cancer. I've got cancer.

There you go. Said it. Done. It's a perfectly normal thing, it's being sorted, I'm going to be alright.'

'Are they treating it?'

'Paraplatin. Chemotherapy, basically. They did a few rounds of that to see if it'd shrink it enough to operate and remove the tumour, but it's borderline apparently. They're pushing for a bigger load of chemo and hoping that'll do the trick.'

'What about… I mean, I would've thought I'd notice the chemotherapy.'

'Don't worry, it's not a wig,' Caroline said, noticing his eyes flicking up towards her hairline. 'Paraplatin rarely causes hair loss. I guess that's why I… Christ, where is he? Maybe we should go inside and wait for him there.'

'You didn't tell Mark either, did you?'

'What? That's a crazy thing to say. Is this definitely the right pub? I spotted another one further up the road. Maybe we should check that one, just in case.'

'That's where you were the other day, isn't it? When Mark came to drop off your lunch but you weren't there. You had the day off and he didn't know. You forgot your lunch because you weren't going to work. You were going to the hospital.'

'Dex, I think we should probably focus on the job in hand. This guy could turn up any minute.'

'And that's why you collapsed. You've been trying to carry on as normal so no-one notices anything's wrong, but it didn't work. You didn't want people to think you couldn't cope.'

'I'm coping fine, Dex. In fact I'm the only one of us who's focusing on what we've come here for.'

'Why haven't you told him?'

Caroline stayed silent for a few moments. There were no words that seemed right.

'It's not as simple as that,' she said eventually. 'I didn't want to hurt them.'

'I think I'd probably be more hurt if my other half had kept something like that from me.'

'Yeah, well, everyone's different. We've all got our reasons.'

They sat in silence for a little while longer before Dexter finally sighed, then spoke.

'He's not turning up, is he?'

50

Dexter drove Caroline home in almost complete silence. She would've preferred to have driven herself, but Mark had taken the car. It was, of course, still absent when she returned home, and she felt strangely sad at seeing the car-less driveway. It was rare she came home to an empty house, and in the light of what had happened it felt even more depressing than usual.

She waved to Dexter and fumbled in her pocket for her house keys. As she did so, she noticed a plant pot had ended up on its side, smashed. The geraniums that'd been on glorious show inside it were scattered on the paving slabs. Must've been a fox or some cats fighting, she thought. She sighed and told herself she'd deal with it in the morning. But her relaxed attitude changed the moment she reached her front door.

Something didn't feel right. She put her key in the lock and turned it, but the door was already unlocked.

She was sure she'd locked it before she left the house. She had, hadn't she?

A sudden thought crossed her mind that Mark might have come back with the boys and let himself in. His car was nowhere to be seen, so it was unlikely, but it was the option she most hoped would be true.

She pushed the door open and called out their names, but got no reply.

The house felt eerily quiet. Caroline flicked the switch on the wall, flooding the hallway with light. Almost immediately, she noticed the footprints.

They were large — definitely a man's — and muddy, too. The length of the stride, leading to the living room and back to the front door again, displayed a clear confidence. Cautiously, she followed them to the living room doorway and peered inside.

Nothing seemed out of place on first sight. She flicked the light switch on and stepped inside, looking around much more carefully now. It was only when she reached the coffee table that she noticed it.

Lying on top of some magazines and bills was something she'd never seen before, but recognised instantly. It was a tourist information leaflet for Normanton Church. She picked it up and opened it, watching as a piece of paper slid out and fell onto the table.

51

Dear Detective Inspector Hills,

    I need you to understand what happened — and why.

    As far as I'm concerned, justice has been done, as best as it can be done. It doesn't even come close to making up for what we lost — those valley communities — but knowing those vile bastards are dead and no longer living off the fruits of our misery is at least some consolation.

    I need you to know what we went through. Houses are not just buildings. They're homes. Everything our families had worked for. Gone. Some of those homes had been passed down through generations. My mother was born in our house. So was I. We knew nothing else. Can you imagine waking up one morning to someone telling *you they were going to knock down your home and you'd have to move? No option. No appeal. Nothing.*

    It's one of my earliest memories, I think. It's certainly the clearest. And it's the only one which hasn't felt any more distant as time has gone on.

    I'm not a bad person. I'm not a murderer, no matter how much I've wanted the Cliftons dead every day of my life since.

When old Arthur Clifton died, I felt joy — briefly. I thought the company would go to the wall like all the others. I hoped, somehow, I'd wake to news of it going bust and hear the entire family had lost all their ill-gotten gains. No such luck.

When Roger Clifton inherited the company, I saw him as the walking embodiment of his grandfather. He'd been around when the valleys were flooded. He'd profited from what had happened, even if it hadn't been his decision. And when I realised I might not see the day his business crumbled and his world fell apart, there was no way I could let that happen. I had to see him suffer, had to see him lose everything.

I hadn't counted on the other brother appearing. When I heard he'd taken on the company, I couldn't sit back and let him profit from the misery of my family and all the others who lost their homes as a result of what his family did. He had to die too.

I don't know what happens now. I don't care all that much. If the wife gets it, fine. She's welcome to it. Rumour is she'd been shagging around behind Roger's back for years anyway, so there's a certain poetic justice in him being six feet under and her living off his money.

You'll want to know exactly what happened, won't you? I have no desire to make life more difficult for you or to hamper your investigation. I've achieved what I needed to achieve. I've had my justice. It's only fair you get yours, too. After all, that's what we both want, isn't it? Justice.

Roger used to go out for evening walks in the country lanes. I know, because I spent quite some time watching his movements. On that Saturday evening, I parked up on one of the lanes, waiting for him. As he walked past my car, I hit him round the back of the head with a crowbar. I dragged him away from the road, into the bushes, just in case anyone came past, and strangled him with a plastic rope until he was dead. Then I dragged him into the boot of my car and waited until it was dark.

I drove to Normanton, broke the lock on the gate with bolt cutters, and took my car right up to the church. I managed to reverse up quite close, then hauled his body up over my shoulder and carried him over to the rocks. I loved the idea of the symbolism of it all, knowing how much he hated religion. One final joke at his expense. Plus, I must admit I thought it might throw you off the scent for a little longer. Sorry.

I was going to wait a day or two for things to die down, then disappear. But then I heard on the grapevine that his brother had turned up. I realised there was a chance he'd inherit the company, and it turned out to be true. At that point, I knew he had to die too. I watched his movements for a few days, but there didn't seem to be much of a pattern. He stayed with Alice Clifton briefly, in Empingham. When I knew he'd spent so much time drinking in the pub, I waited for him. I was parked a little further up the road from the house. When he got there, I did exactly the same to him as I did to his brother. Then I drove home.

I had some things I needed to put in place after that. Some final arrangements. But now they're done.

By the time you read this and have worked out who I am, I'll be gone. The final part of my plan will be complete.

At that point, finally, I'll be truly happy.

52

Caroline's hands were shaking as she phoned Dexter, and she was relieved to find he had his phone hooked up to the car's speakers. She explained the situation — that someone had been in her house and she was almost certain it was the killer — and Dexter turned around immediately and headed back to her.

She was waiting on the front doorstep when he arrived. The footsteps showed the intruder had already left, but she still didn't feel safe in the house.

Between them, they scoured the house from top to bottom, making absolutely sure there was no-one there. Every room, every cupboard, every corner of the attic, until Caroline's heartbeat had returned to normal and she could tell herself quite reasonably and logically that there was no-one else in the house.

She didn't have a spare lock, and had no idea how the intruder had managed to unlock that one in any case. Dexter said he suspected it had been picked and that she should invest in a better lock — something Caroline immediately bumped up to the top of the growing home improvements list.

When Dexter left, taking the letter with him, she locked the door and left the key in, pulled the security chain across and wedged one of Archie's toys under the handle to add an extra layer of security. She knew she wouldn't sleep well tonight, and wondered if she should even bother trying. With nothing else to do, and wanting to hear a safe and familiar voice, she picked up her phone and FaceTimed Mark.

'Hey you,' Mark said as he answered, his characteristic smile on his face.

'Hi. How's things? How are the boys?'

'Yeah, all good. Think they're starting to get a bit edgy. I forgot to mention to them that Grandma doesn't have an Xbox.'

Caroline laughed. 'Yeah, I wondered how long they'd manage without Minecraft.'

'Oh no, don't worry. Josh managed to get hold of that on his phone.'

'Course he did.' Caroline had silently cursed their decision to allow Josh to have his first phone recently, but her job meant she knew the advantages and disadvantages. Knowing where Josh was at all times was key, as was his ability to get in touch with them should he need to — especially after the bullying he'd endured at his last school in London. These days, parental controls and security settings were easy to lock down, and on balance she felt it had been the right decision.

She felt safer now, speaking to Mark, knowing there was no-one else in the house and anyone trying to get in would struggle to do so. Logically, she understood the intruder wouldn't break in with her there. That was why he'd waited until she'd left the house earlier that evening. Indeed, she now felt certain Edward Picton was their man and that he hadn't intended to visit the Wheatsheaf at Greetham at all, but had been playing them all along, and had instead broken into her house and left that letter on her coffee table.

'You look… better,' Mark said, pulling her back to the here and now.

'Do I?' She couldn't see any conceivable way in which the last few hours would've made her look better than she had before.

'Yeah. You look less… I dunno. Stressed. You seem more relaxed.'

She didn't feel it, but that wasn't something she was about to admit. She wondered if perhaps opening up to Dexter had lifted a weight from her shoulders. The biggest burden still needed to be shifted, but she was pleased Mark had noticed a change.

'Thanks,' she said. 'Maybe a bit of time and space is all we need sometimes.'

'I was thinking maybe we might come back first thing instead of in the evening tomorrow. Roads'll be hell later on, with the rest of the bank holiday traffic. Plus the boys are missing you already.'

'I miss them too.'

She dearly wanted to open up to Mark, but this wasn't the time or the place. She needed him to be here with her.

Tomorrow night, she promised herself, was when she'd tell him everything.

She said her goodbyes, then put the phone down on the coffee table. She needed to swallow her emotions for another day. She'd done it for years already, so what was another few hours?

She felt nervous at the thought of having to tell him everything, but accepted it was for the best. Keeping things to herself hadn't worked, and this was the only option she had left. Then she could worry about her job, and whether she'd even have one once this was all over. She had a distinct feeling she'd be left on paperwork duties, or that some decree would come from above that anything more serious than a cat stuck up a tree would be handed straight over to EMSOU. And that was before she even started to worry about the chemotherapy.

There were too many things to worry about. Work provided her the focus and structure she needed to get through things. And in that moment, she knew what she had to do. She headed over to the pile of papers and documents Dexter had brought over, opened her laptop and got to work.

53

There was something comforting about not being constrained by the very specific and process-driven way things were done in the Met. It got results — that couldn't be denied — but Caroline wasn't sure it was any more successful than the holistic approach to policing she preferred.

This was much more like the job she'd envisaged, spending a late Sunday evening hunched over a laptop and a pile of papers, crossing the t's and dotting the i's and trying to find a crack somewhere — anywhere — which might provide her with a breakthrough.

As she flicked through the sheets of paper and read the notes left by Dexter, Sara and Aidan, she felt immensely proud of her little team. They were severely under-resourced in comparison to other major incident teams, and the thought of a team of four solving a double-murder case was practically unthinkable. Even a simple house burglary tended to involve a much larger team in most other forces.

This was precisely why major cases tended to be handed over to their colleagues in EMSOU.

She moved a pile of papers to one side, knocking a small object to the floor. She recognised it immediately as a USB stick. She put it in her laptop and waited for it to be recognised. As soon as she opened the folder, she noticed the name, which told her it was the CCTV footage from outside the library in Oakham.

She loaded up the files and played them, skipping through to the time the death threat had been emailed to Roger Clifton. The footage was from inside the library. And as she watched, a cold chill ran down her spine.

Her first thought was that Sara had clearly made a mistake. Caroline knew exactly who the person on the tape was. How had Sara not spotted him? But then the horrible truth dawned on her. Sara had never met this man. He'd never even been a suspect. Her heart thumped heavily in her chest as it all started to make sense and she realised she was staring at their killer.

54

It seemed to take an age for Dexter to answer his phone, but in reality it was only a few seconds.

'Dex, I know who it is. I know who killed Roger and Arthur Clifton.'

Dexter was silent for a moment. 'Right… Who?'

'Howard Smallwood. And no, it's not another one of my wild theories. It all makes perfect sense.'

'Smallwood? The history guy?'

'Yes. He was on CCTV using his laptop in the library around the time that email was sent to Roger Clifton. He knew all about the history of the area and what had happened. Of course he did. It's literally what he does. He was at the scene that morning, too, remember? The first time we met him, he stopped us as we came out of the Waterside Cafe. He knew we were police officers and he couldn't help but give us his two cents. He's been toying with us all along. Dex, how closely did you look at that list of families who were displaced from the Hambletons?'

'Uh, well, not that closely. Sara and Aidan were doing most of the checking and cross-referencing.'

'Exactly. And Sara and Aidan never met or contacted Howard Smallwood, did they? You and I met him at the Waterside Cafe. You and I met him in Otters. I doubt Sara and Aidan even knew his name. He was certainly never a name that was mentioned as a suspect, so why would they think anything of seeing him on the list of displaced families?'

'You're joking.'

'I wish I was. But it gets even more tragic than that. "Mrs Annie Smallwood plus one boy, seven."'

'Howard Smallwood was seven years old?'

'So it seems. And there was only him and his mother.'

'So he's not even sixty? Christ, he hasn't aged well.'

'That's what a lifetime of bitterness and anger does to you. Seven's an impressionable age for boys, trust me. He lost his family home, the house his mother had been bringing him up in single-handed. That's going to leave one hell of a scar. There's your motive. He said it himself in his letter. Kill the only remaining people responsible. Or, at least, responsible in his mind. We've got him at the scene of the murder, plus evidence of him sending a death threat to Roger Clifton a week and a half before he's murdered.'

'But why now? Roger and Arthur were only boys themselves when the villages were flooded. In fact, I don't think Arthur was even born, was he?'

'No, not until a year or two after. But a seven-year-old boy can't go around committing murder, can he? Maybe the bitterness and anger built up too much over the years. He saw them as the continuation of Arthur Clifton Construction and held them responsible.'

'But he could've done it at any point in his adult life, surely? Why wait until he's pushing sixty and starting to slo… Oh, fuck.'

'What?'

'Fuck.'

'Dex, talk to me.'

'When we met Smallwood at Otters, he made some comment about a lump on his brain that was ready to kill him. I think he called it an olive. I didn't think anything of it at the time, but do you remember what he said on the phone the other day? He said he was going away late Sunday night, so we'd have to be quick. He wasn't talking about coming to him with research questions. It was a direct challenge to us to catch him. A deadline. He's going away. Tonight. He's going away to die.'

'Oh shit.' Caroline praised Dexter's memory and keen eye for detail, although right now it had caused her more stress and anxiety than she'd felt in a long time. She looked at the clock. 'Shit. Shit. We need to find him. Now. Where does he live?'

'I don't know. But we can find out. I'll make a call now and get vehicle licensing to check his name locally. There'll be something somewhere.'

'Good. Go,' she said, hanging up the call.

Caroline paced the room, all the little details falling into place in her mind. How had she been so stupid? She'd naively believed Howard Smallwood to be a harmless — if a little eccentric — history buff. There was no way she'd ever have had him down as a double murderer, but all the signs were there, right from the start. He'd seemed keen, but she'd presumed that was just one of his eccentricities, his social awkwardness. He'd even made a point of telling them to get in touch with him if ever they needed—

Yes! The business card! Caroline took the stairs two at a time and headed into her bedroom, going straight over to the pile of receipts, parking stickers and cards that covered the top of her dressing table, ready for their quarterly sort-and-file. Her hands shook with adrenaline as she quickly rummaged through them until she saw the one she wanted. Howard Smallwood's business card.

She looked at the address and did a quick bit of mental maths. Smallwood lived in Oakham, but the opposite side of town. Mark still had the car, and Dexter would be a good half an hour, even if he left immediately and put his foot down. She ran back downstairs, put on her comfiest shoes and sprinted as fast as she could.

55

Her legs felt like lead and the air burned in her lungs, but she had to keep pushing forwards. She'd never been the most gifted athlete, but it was amazing what a decent burst of adrenaline could do.

As she sprinted down Station Road, past the train station and Station Approach leading to the Grainstore Brewery, she saw the barriers coming down across the main road, signalling that a train was coming. There had to be another way across. There must be. All she knew from sitting in traffic trying to cross the tracks on countless occasions was that the trains took absolutely ages to pass through.

She felt her phone vibrating in her pocket, and wondered how long it had been ringing for. She took it out and saw Dexter's name on the screen.

'Dex,' she said, panting.

'I've got the address.'

'I know. Me too. On his business card.'

'Are you okay? You sound really out of breath.'

'I'm on my way.'

'Don't. It's too dangerous. I've put in a call and there are officers on the way. No idea how long they'll be, though. I'm in the car too, going as fast as I can. Whatever you do, don't go in there.'

'I have to. We can't wait. We're going to lose him.'

'It's too risky. For the sake of a few extra minutes, we can't take risks like that.'

'This is his deadline, Dex. His countdown. This was his plan all along.'

'Please. Stop. Listen, it's not just the driver licensing database Smallwood was on. He's got a gun licence, too. He owns hunting rifles. Firearms are coming over from Leicester. Just wait. It's too dangerous.'

She tensed at his words, knowing and understanding the risks, but at the same time unable to let go. Howard Smallwood's actions had consumed her for two weeks. He'd made her sicker than she'd ever been. He'd ruined her marriage, almost ended her career.

Caroline looked ahead and saw the footbridge on the other side of the main road, rising up over the train line and back down onto the Cold Overton Road on the other side of the tracks.

'Dex, I've got to go. I'll see you there.'

56

Howard Smallwood lived in a quiet street off the Braunston Road — not that any streets in Oakham were particularly lively at this time on a Sunday night.

Caroline put her hand in her pocket and pulled out his business card again, looking at the number to make sure she'd got it right. She had. Number six. Third house up on the right.

As she approached, she wondered if she should wait for her colleagues, but she knew time was of the essence. There was no sign of any police cars — nor of Dexter. She looked at her watch. There was no way he'd be here for a little while yet.

The fact the light was on meant Smallwood was likely still at home. She could wait here — *should* wait here — and keep an eye on the house until backup arrived. But at the same time she felt the unavoidable urge to go inside.

She wasn't even on the case anymore. She didn't have to wait for backup. She didn't have to follow the procedure.

But it wasn't just about procedure. It was about the truth. It was about justice. Smallwood had brought her to her knees. The case had consumed her for two weeks — two weeks when her health, her marriage and her job were at their most fragile, and he'd almost finished her. There was no way in hell she was going to let some plod from Leicester with a helmet wade in and take the glory. She had to face Smallwood herself, look him in the eye and meet her adversary. After he'd come so close to defeating her, that was a moment she would relish.

Caroline walked up the short driveway of number six, stopping on the doorstep for a moment to catch her breath, then she tried the door handle. It was unlocked.

It was only thirty seconds later, once she was in Howard Smallwood's kitchen, that she heard the cocking of a gun.

57

'Down on your knees. No sudden moves, alright?' Smallwood said, his voice almost a whisper. He was trying to sound calm, but Caroline could tell he was shitting bricks. That wasn't ideal — not when he had a gun in his hand.

'What's this all about, Howard? Why the gun?'

'Why not?'

'Because it doesn't fit. The clues. The little remarks. You wanted us to find you, didn't you?'

'I wondered if you would. It doesn't mean I wanted you to, though.'

'So what was it? Was it the challenge? The thrill of the chase?' Caroline knew that as long as she kept him talking, she'd be delaying things, giving the firearms officers more time to get to Oakham from Leicester. She didn't want to die. Not here. Not now.

'If you like.'

No, no, keep talking. Keep talking.

'Did you break into my house tonight?'

'Why, did you think it might've been a particularly keen tourist information manager?'

Out of the corner of her eye, she could see the clock on the front of Smallwood's oven. She was acutely aware she had to fill a lot of time if she was going to stand a chance of getting out of here alive.

'You used to live in the Hambletons, didn't you?'

'That's no secret. I'm amazed it took you as long as it did to find out.'

'I can't imagine how hard it must have been to have gone through that, at that age. Losing your home. Being moved from the place you knew and loved, all because someone else told you to.'

'That cottage was my grandmother's. She was born there. So was my mum. It was ours. No-one else's.'

'I know. Things... things that happen at that age stick with you.'

'Don't try to psychoanalyse me. You won't manage it, trust me.'

'I'm not. Honestly, I'm not. What I'm saying is you and I probably aren't as different as you might think.'

'Oh, so now you want to be my friend. Now you're kneeling on my kitchen floor with a gun to your head.'

Caroline glanced at the clock again. 'It's not about friends and enemies, Howard. It's about shared experiences. I've... I've been there. Not exactly the same, but still a traumatic event at a young age. I... I had a brother.' She felt a sudden surge of something inside her, a welling up of emotions she hadn't addressed or spoken about for decades. 'There was a... Something happened. Something that shouldn't have happened. Something that could have been avoided. He died. And the worst thing is he didn't need to. I... I've had to live with that all my life.' The words tumbled out of her as the tears rolled silently down her cheeks. 'I know you're not going to believe me, but I've genuinely never told anyone this. Not for years. I don't even know why I'm telling you, but here we are. I am. But that's what happens, isn't it? Things that should be buried, and which are buried for years, always bubble up to the surface. Nothing stays down. There's only so long you can hide things and hope they'll go away. Because they don't, do they? And sooner or later something happens which means you've got no choice but to act on whatever it is you've repressed. And the feelings you should've dealt with years ago have to be dealt with in other ways. Is that why you did this now? Because of the tumour?'

'We're not here to talk about that. You know nothing.'

'Trust me, I know far more than you think I do. I've got one too. On one of my ovaries. I've been having chemothcrapy, but it hasn't shrunk it enough. They're talking about operating, but I don't know. There's so much going through my mind, I don't know what to do or what's going to happen.'

Smallwood was silent for a moment before speaking. 'At least you've got a choice.'

'Tell me,' she whispered. She could hear his breathing getting heavier with emotion.

'Glioblastoma. The most aggressive form of brain cancer. I'm at stage four. Same as the percentage of people who survive it. And those are the ones who get treatment.'

'Are they not treating you?'

'There's no point. Most people are dead within a year. You know, when a doctor tells you that, you get this sense that you're going to gradually get worse, but never really know when the end will be. What they don't tell you is that you can absolutely feel the end coming. It's why animals go somewhere safe and alone to die. They know what's happening. Their body tells them.'

'Is that what you planned to do? You said you were going away tonight.'

'We all have our safe place. The spot where we want to finally be laid to rest.'

'Can I ask?'

'What difference will it make? You'll only try and stop me.'

'I'm not at liberty to stop anything right now, Howard. You're pointing a hunting rifle at the back of my head.'

Caroline heard a gentle clatter as Smallwood put the gun on the kitchen table.

'Go on, then. Arrest me. Deny a man his final resting place.'

'Howard, even if I let you go you'd be stopped at the border.'

'Border of what? I'm not leaving the country. I'm not even leaving the county.'

Caroline closed her eyes and nodded. 'Rutland Water.'

'Nether Hambleton.'

'You're planning to drown yourself?'

'Sleeping tablets. I'm going to row out to the right spot with ballast tied to me. Some lighter fluid. A pack of matches. And just as I'm drifting off, with my last bit of energy, I strike the match. I won't feel a thing. I'll be long gone. So will the boat. And I'll be pulled down by the ballast. Back home.'

There was something in the way he spoke that tugged at Caroline's heartstrings. He sounded like a young boy. A lost boy. And in that moment, she had an overwhelming urge to step aside and let him go. After all, what was there to lose? He wasn't going to get away with anything. Within a few hours he'd be dead and lying at the bottom of Rutland Water, exactly where his childhood home had once been. What good would it do anyone for him to die a few weeks or months later in a prison cell somewhere? If he was as gravely ill as he said, he probably wouldn't even make it as far as the trial. But that feeling didn't last long.

Bubbling away underneath it was that anger at everything Howard Smallwood's perverse little game had put her through over the past two weeks. Everything she'd lost or nearly lost. Everything that had been put at risk. She looked over towards him, watching him lost in his reverie. And before he could react, she launched herself at him.

58

He was stronger than she thought. Far stronger. She'd heard stories of people who'd found superhuman strength when faced with a battle they absolutely had to win. Deep, primal urges were real, and they were strong.

She tried to put an arm around his neck and get him into a headlock, but she couldn't reach quickly enough. Smallwood pushed back, catching her off balance and sending her backwards, her spine crashing into the edge of the kitchen work surface.

She shouldn't have thrown herself at him. She should have kept him calm, kept him quiet, kept him talking until backup arrived. There were always plenty of things she should have done but didn't. It was the story of her life.

Now the challenge was to keep him at bay, fend him off and restrain him until the firearms officers turned up. She had a feeling there'd be a whole new battle then, but that wouldn't be her responsibility. Besides which, that was easier said than done.

Smallwood charged at her, far too quickly for her to move out of the way, and she felt her back crush against the edge of the worktop again, sending bolts of pain down through her legs. She tried to stumble forward to throw him off balance, but her legs didn't have the strength. They'd gone dead.

She fell to her knees and grasped at Smallwood, trying to rugby tackle him to the ground, but he'd already shifted his weight on top of her. As he turned round to push her face-down on the floor, she slammed her right elbow backwards, catching him square in the chest.

It gave her a couple of seconds of breathing space, but it wasn't enough. In that instant, she remembered the rifle. She reached up to grab it, but saw Smallwood's hand reach it first, before it disappeared out of sight.

His knee and lower leg came down on her back, pinning her face-first on the ground as she felt the cold barrel of the rifle press against the back of her head.

'It wasn't meant to end like this. I promise,' Smallwood said, before pulling the trigger.

59

The click was only gentle, but Caroline reacted as if a bomb had gone off. A moment or two later, though, she realised she could still hear the sound of her own breathing.

A second click.

Before her brain could come to the conclusion that the gun had failed to fire, she felt a sudden searing pain as Smallwood slammed the butt of the rifle into the back of her head, leaving her wailing and writhing in agony.

The instinct to try and get to her feet hadn't even reached her as Smallwood wrapped his arm around her neck and pulled backwards, tensing his muscles as his arm began to crush her windpipe.

A sudden moment of clarity came to her. This was how it ended. This was how it had ended for Roger and Arthur Clifton, and it was how it would end for her too. The blow to the back of the head, then strangulation.

In that moment, all she could think of was Mark and the boys, sitting around his mum's dinner table, laughing and joking, oblivious to the fact she was about to become Howard Smallwood's latest — final — victim.

She'd never realised how much the human throat could collapse under pressure. There was no way of getting air into her lungs. No way of releasing Smallwood's grip. She felt the blood throb in her head as it struggled to circulate, her lungs desperately gasping for air.

As her vision started to speckle and blacken around the edges, she realised this was it. This was the end.

60

The air rushed into Caroline's lungs as she wheezed and coughed. That sweet oxygen couldn't come quickly enough, and her chest burned as her vision started to come back to her.

She had no idea how long she'd been out, or what had happened between then and now, but Smallwood was no longer on top of her. His arm was no longer around her throat.

She could hear sounds of a struggle, the noise of people shouting. The blood throbbed in her temples as it restored its usual journey through her veins.

She rolled onto her back, still gasping for air, which couldn't come quickly enough. She turned her head to the side and saw Dexter pinning Smallwood to the ground, his knee and lower leg on Smallwood's back as he held his wrists behind him.

'You okay?' Dexter said

Caroline nodded, her neck stiff and sore. She didn't try

to speak. Didn't want to speak. In any case, there were no words she could possibly say. Her job had always shown her how fragile life could be and how quickly and easily it could be snuffed out. Those were facts she knew, but which she'd never experienced in quite that way. Not for many years, anyway.

She looked at Smallwood and was disturbed to see his face carried no emotion. This was the face of a man resigned to his fate, a man who knew what was coming and still didn't mind one bit. This was how life was always going to turn out for him. This was his fate.

'It's alright,' Dexter said. 'You're safe. You're going to be alright. We've got him. Just hold on. Not long now. We've got him.'

Her head throbbed, but the cold tiles of Howard Smallwood's kitchen floor provided some small relief. From here, her line of sight carried on out of the kitchen door, down the hallway and to the glazed front door. She heard the sound of sirens approaching; that familiar, welcome sound. She felt her eyelids getting heavier as the sound grew louder.

Then came the blue lights, flashing and strobing, bouncing off the frosted glass of Howard Smallwood's front door, lighting the house.

Caroline closed her eyes and waited.

61

Caroline had never expected to spend her Monday morning in a hospital bed, but it would be fair to say the last couple of weeks hadn't conformed to expectations in many ways.

A thousand thoughts swirled around her head as she woke up. Where were Mark and the boys? What happened to Smallwood? Was Dexter okay? What about her job? She was certain it wouldn't go down well once her superiors found out she'd gone to Smallwood's house alone, even though she'd been taken off the case. But in that moment, she didn't care. She was alive.

'Has anyone ever told you you look ridiculous when you're asleep?'

She didn't need to turn her head, because she recognised the voice immediately. She let out half-laugh, half-sigh. 'Thanks, Dex.'

'No, seriously. Your mouth sort of hangs open like a fish, but only a little bit. When you breath in and out your lips kinda click and pop. It's weird.'

'Spoken like a true failed doctor. Don't tell me — you finally passed the exams so they let you treat me.'

'You wish. I'm only here because I didn't fancy taking the rap from Arnold. I'm not going anywhere near the office until I've got you in front of me as a human shield.'

'What happened to Smallwood?'

'He's in the nick.'

'Leicester?'

'Yup. No skin off our nose. Saves us having to look at him again. It's a bit of poetic justice, in a way. He wanted to end his days in Rutland. Now he's stuck in a prison cell in Leicester. Can't beat bad luck, can you?'

'I'm sure Leicester's lovely.'

'Yeah, well you did take quite a knock to the head. Apparently he's made a full confession. Nothing to lose, I guess. There's a decent chance he won't even make it to trial.'

'Judging by the strength he showed last night, I think he's got a fair bit left in the tank yet.'

'Silent killer, apparently.'

'Him or the brain tumour?'

Dexter laughed. 'At least it means there's some closure. And in even better news, Patrick Walsh thinks you're only the second-biggest dick in Rutland. Turns out Smallwood had got wind of his affair with Alice Clifton from watching the family's movements and thought it'd be a fun little twist to his game if he implicated Walsh. I think he just wanted to fuck up the entire family.'

'It's not just the one family, though, is it? What he did spreads so much further than that.'

'Regroup, rebuild and whatever the other R-word is.'

'Listen, Dex, if I end up getting let go, I just want you to know I'm really grateful for everything you've done. Not just with Smallwood, but… you know.'

'You won't be going anywhere. Whatever goes down on paper, the fact is it was you who worked out it was Smallwood. If it wasn't for you, he'd be lying at the bottom of Rutland Water right now, having died an innocent man.'

'Fingers crossed Arnold sees it like that.'

'He'll be alright.'

'Sorry.'

'You've got nothing to apologise for. I mean, maybe you could loosen the reins a little and listen a bit more to what other people have to say, but I think we can let you have at least an hour of glory first.'

'Oh yeah, I feel properly glorious lying here.'

'You don't look it,' said a voice from the doorway. It was Mark, with Josh and Archie standing beside him. 'How are you feeling?'

'Never been better. Is anything actually wrong with me?'

'Observations,' Dexter said. 'They're probably looking for a heart.'

'You're on fine form this morning, Dex.'

'Not enough coffee. On which note, I'll leave you lot to it for a bit. Nice to see you again, Mark.'

'You too, mate.' Mark watched Dexter leave, then walked over to Caroline, leaned over and hugged her. 'Come on, boys. Give your mum a hug.'

She found it impossible to put into words how much she'd missed them. They'd only been gone a couple of days, but it felt so much longer. A lot had happened, and the fact she'd almost lost her life a few hours earlier hadn't escaped her notice.

'What happened? We didn't get any info, except to say you'd been injured arresting someone and taken to hospital. They said it wasn't serious and not to worry, but we jumped straight in the car first thing anyway.'

'Yeah, it's fine. It was nothing,' Caroline said. 'Actually, we'll talk about it later. Just a bit knackered now. But we'll talk. I promise. And you two,' she said, pulling her sons in close again, 'will be pleased to know I'm going to take a bit of time off to spend with you.'

She looked over the top of their heads and at Mark. For the first time in a long time, she could see warmth in his eyes.

62

Although she'd been signed off by the doctor later that morning, it wasn't until seven o'clock that she was finally discharged and allowed to leave the hospital. By the time they got home, the boys were already knackered from their early start and long day, so Caroline flaked out on the sofa while Mark put them to bed upstairs. She'd barely settled in when the doorbell rang.

She got up, opened the door and was surprised to see Detective Superintendent Derek Arnold standing on her doorstep.

'Evening. Hope I'm not disturbing you. I heard you'd been sent home, so wanted to see how you were.'

'Yeah, I'm alright. You know how it is. Come in,' she said, looking forward to sitting back on the sofa again, rather than spending the next few minutes standing at the door.

'You've got a week off — more if you need it and the doctors tell you to. Just so you know, you'll be invited to a meeting with me when you get back. And yes, I will be giving you a proper dressing down. Got to be like that on paper, anyway.'

'And what about not on paper?'

'Well, you're not losing your job if that's what you're asking. I think it'll probably be an official warning, but again, that's on paper. Between you and me, yes, I think it was a bloody stupid idea to do what you did, but I can see why you did it.'

'Honestly, we wouldn't have caught him otherwise. I genuinely believe that.'

'I know. I'm sure it'll all come out in the wash. But that's not to say changes don't need to be made. I think you and I both know this hasn't been handled in the best way. Product of the system, perhaps. But systems are there to be changed and improved.'

Caroline felt a surge of dread in the pit of her stomach.

'You're not suggesting all major crimes go through EMSOU, are you?'

'No. No, of course not. At least, that's not *my* intention. There are others who might disagree with that, though. That's why you're probably going to have to explain your actions to a panel and undergo some sort of extra training.'

She dearly wanted to remind him that she'd been a senior investigating officer in the Met and had more experience dealing with major crimes than every officer in Rutland combined, but it didn't seem worth the hassle. She was happy to have kept hold of her job. For her, that was the main thing.

'We'll probably have to work a little more closely, you

and I,' Arnold said. 'We definitely don't need a loose cannon knocking about. Not with people leaning down our necks from up above, not to mention EMSOU. I know you do a good job. I know Smallwood would have died an innocent man if you hadn't done what you did. But we've still got to make sure things are done properly. By the book, if you like.'

'On paper, at least?'

Arnold smiled. 'Yes. On paper, at least.'

63

Once Derek Arnold had gone, Caroline and Mark sat back down.

'Would you like a drink?' Mark asked.

'God, yes please.'

'I imagine you'll want something a bit stronger tonight.'

'Definitely.'

'Actually, I think there's a bottle of gin in the kitchen. I'll go and grab that.'

'Oh. No. Maybe not that. On second thoughts, let's just stick to wine.'

When Mark had come back with a bottle and two glasses, Caroline decided she needed to get straight to the point. There was no point delaying things any further. He'd waited long enough. She'd spent the whole day trying to think of words that might work, rolling them around in her mind, trying her hardest to put her thoughts together in a coherent stream that he might understand. But she didn't know if he ever would.

She hoped she hadn't done too much damage. She couldn't change the fact she'd hidden her illness from him, and lying about that would only make things worse. Now was the time for honesty. With any luck, they'd be able to draw a line under what had happened and move forward.

'Mark, I need to tell you something. I've not been well recently. For quite a while, actually. I don't know why I didn't tell you. I should have. But the longer it went on, the harder it was. That's why I wasn't at work that day when you brought my lunch in. It's why I've been sick sometimes. And tired. And irritable. But it's being sorted. I'll be alright.'

Mark nodded slowly. 'When you say not well…'

'Cancer. Ovarian. They caught it early, though. They're confident.' She looked up at Mark and could see the colour had drained from his face. 'I wanted to tell you, but there was so much going on and all I wanted to do was protect you. Honestly, the only thing on my mind was you and the boys. Nothing else. Nothing at all. It was stupid of me, I know, but I thought I could get it sorted without worrying you or anyone else. I know it sounds ridiculous to say it now, but it's true. I didn't want to hurt any of you. I just wanted you all to be happy and not worry. I thought I could sort it out on my own.'

'How long have you known?' he whispered.

Caroline could see the hurt on his face and she knew it would take some time for them to rebuild. But it was out there now. She'd been honest. She'd opened up and told him the truth. For her, that was a huge step forward.

She opened her mouth and began to talk. A few minutes

later, she closed her eyes and waited for his response. She'd told him everything. Nearly everything.

ON BORROWED TIME
BOOK #2 IN THE RUTLAND CRIME SERIES

Each morning, the first train of the day leaves Oakham station and thunders through a tunnel under the village of Manton. But today the driver sees something that changes his life: A dead body hangs in the tunnel's exit.

DI Caroline Hills knows this isn't a suicide. It's murder. And when a second apparent suicide appears in Rutland, Caroline uncovers a shocking link: the victims knew each other.

As Rutland Police fight to catch the killer, a group of friends is left with an even more shocking realisation. One of them is the murderer. And one of them will be the next to die.

———

'Incredible' — *BBC News*

'A sensation' — *The Guardian*

———

Out 29th September 2020

Available to pre-order now.

ACKNOWLEDGMENTS

Well, you either stuck through it to the end or you've skipped to this page in an attempt to find out who the killer is without having to read it. If it's the former, thank you. If it's the latter, my apologies; you need to flick back a few pages.

I should make an admission. Rutland Police doesn't actually exist. There. I've said it. My dirty secret is out. In reality, crime in Rutland (of which there is very little) is dealt with admirably and very capably by Leicestershire Police, who maintain small departments in Oakham and Uppingham, one of which I have shamelessly re-appropriated as a much more in-depth headquarters for my fictional Rutland Police.

In fact, I've taken many liberties when it comes to the policing and procedure, as I do in most of my books. There's an old adage I can't be bothered to Google that basically says it's better to learn everything and choose what not to use than to go in ignorantly. When it comes to police procedure and detail that I've learnt and chosen not to use — or, more likely, forgotten — I owe a great debt of thanks to the numerous serving and ex-police officers who have helped me over the years and continue to do so now.

Much of my policing knowledge has come from David Parry, a former detective with Leicestershire Police, who helped me get my procedure on track many years before I ever imagined setting a book on his doorstep.

More recently, my friend and ex-Chief Superintendent Graham Bartlett has got me out of numerous holes and suggested a number of ways in which I could improve the police procedure and, ultimately, stories I write.

To those serving police officers who'd rather remain nameless but are nonetheless incredibly patient and helpful in response to my endless text messages and daft questions, thank you.

The fact is real-life policing is actually quite dull. I'm well aware no-one wants to read books about huge teams of people doing endless shift work, suffering office politics and growing piles of paperwork (and if you do, you really must get a life). Of course, story must win out. I hope I've at least managed to nail that bit.

Writing a book which is heavily location-based is always a challenge, especially when you don't live in the area you're writing about. Doing so under a government lockdown due to a global pandemic makes it a touch trickier still. Being unable to visit Rutland whilst writing this book certainly provided me with a challenge, and if I've come close to meeting it, praise should certainly not be directed at me.

My unwavering thanks on that front must go to everyone

who's helped me from afar, answering inane questions about gates, footpaths and countless other minutiae concerning Rutland. In no particular order, these are:

Jill Kimber, Robert Ovens and everyone else at the Rutland Local History & Record Society for the wealth of information they provided me. At this point, I must stress that the Rutland Local History & Record Society is a wonderful, esteemed and incredibly helpful bunch of people, and is an entirely separate entity from the fictional history society mentioned in this book. The Rutland Local History & Record Society has, so far as I know it, no murderers among its ranks, nor should murderers be encouraged to join (although membership is a very reasonable £14 a year, or just £16 for your entire murderous family).

In all seriousness, the RLH&RS is an absolutely superb organisation and a wonderful group of people, and anyone with even a passing interest in the history of Rutland should absolutely become a member.

Jonathan Young, Anglian Water's manager at Rutland Water, was a great help in giving me ideas for how my killer could access Normanton Church under cover of darkness. Thank you, Jonathan.

To the Reverend Canon Leo Osborn for having been willing — but unable — to appear as a character in this book due to his retirement from the clergy, which would have left me looking rather daft had I not realised. Thank you.

To everyone in Rutland who's expressed such a keen enthusiasm for this series, I really cannot thank you enough.

Your passion and interest spurs me on more than you'll ever know, and I hope beyond anything else that I've done your part of the world justice.

I'm sure I've forgotten many of you, but I'm going to have a crack at it anyway. Huge thanks to Beverley Graham for her local knowledge and contacts; to Matt Smith, Ady Dayman, Sophie Price, Namrata Varia and Ben Jackson from BBC Radio Leicestershire; Rob Persani and Jennifer Lee from Rutland Radio; Kerry Coupe — editor of the Rutland & Stamford Mercury; Darren Greenwood from Oakham Nub News and Sue Parslow from The Village Diary magazine for their enthusiasm and keenness to help promote the series.

Huge thanks to all the local business owners and shopkeepers who've been in touch, keen to stock the series and help promote it. In no particular order, and doubtless missing plenty of names because there are still emails coming in as I write this (and I've got to send it off now), thanks to Tim Walker at Walkers bookshop in Oakham and Stamford; Robin Carter at Hygge; and Kristy, Chris, Katie and everyone at the Wisteria Hotel.

Thanks also to Joe Lloyd, a real-life Oakham police officer for providing some laughs and chuckles on Twitter. I'll make sure you get at least a strong cameo in the series!

I must also thank my mum and dad, firstly for introducing me to Rutland and subsequently costing me an arm and a leg in petrol every fortnight, and secondly for putting up with my incessant 'can you just pop down to Normanton and check this' requests. I promise every single 'outsider living in Rutland' joke was aimed squarely at you.

In fact, my dad makes a cameo appearance in this book. If you ever visit Rutland and stay at the Wisteria Hotel, make sure to wave at the doddery old gardener as you walk past.

While I'm warning you about people in pubs, hello to Paul, Tim and John. If you ever bump into a chap in Oakham who insists Dexter was named after his dog, just nod and smile.

Thank you to all the book bloggers and reviewers who are always so eager to read my new books and help promote them: Emily Ellis, Terry Sullivan, Shell Baker, Yvonne Bastian, Nicki Murphy, Jill Burkinshaw, Jo Robertson, Louise Cannon, Alyson Read, Linda Strong, Karen Cocking and all the other people I've undoubtedly missed.

Huge thanks go to Jo Clarke for the information, advice and guidance on types of cancer and their relevant treatments. I always wondered why I was friends with a nurse who had such a deep-seated — and frankly worrying — fascination with cancer, and after nearly twenty years I finally have the answer.

Wedgies and BCG punches to Mark Boutros, for always asking the right questions and getting the most out of my characters. Whenever I'm at the 'bugger it, that'll do' stage, Mark always pushes me on to the next level and ensures everything I write is infinitely better than it otherwise would've been. Why he doesn't inject as much quality into his own writing is anyone's guess.

To Caitlin White, who helped transform my ideas and nonsense into a coherent, thrilling plot and has been an incredible sounding board. Thank you for everything you've done and for having confidence in the series. I'm so pleased you're by my side on this and stopping me from cocking things up.

As always, huge thanks to Lucy Hayward for her feedback and suggestions on this book and my others. They are all much, much better books for it, and I can't thank her enough.

To Xander and Jim, my dashing assistants who undertake a multitude of tasks for me on a daily basis and allow me to just about keep my head above water — thank you.

Of course, I need to thank my wife, Joanne, for talking plots and characters through with me and getting me on the right line on more than one occasion. And for the countless nights in Oakham's wonderful pubs while I was 'doing some research'.

But my biggest thanks, as always, go to you — my readers — and especially those subscribed to my Patreon program. Active supporters get a number of benefits, including the chance of having a character named after them in my books. In *What Lies Beneath*, Barbara Tallis and Peter Tottman were named after Patreon supporters.

If you're interested in becoming a patron, please head over to patreon.com/adamcroft. Your support is enormously valuable.

With that, I'd like to give my biggest thanks to my small but growing group of readers who are currently signed up as Patreon supporters at the time of writing: Ann Sidey, Astrid Rohrlach, Barbara Tallis, Carla Powell, Darren Ashworth, Dawn Blythe, Debbie Rowan, Elaine Smith,

Emiliana Anna Perrone, Emily Ellis, Estelle Golding, Geraldine Rue, Helen Weir, Jeanette Moss, Judy Hopkins, Julie Devonald Cornelius, Karina Gallagher, Leigh Hansen, Linda Anderson, Lisa Bayliss, Lisa Lewkowicz, Louise Ross, Lynne Davis, Lynne Lester-George, Mandy Davies, Maureen Hutchings, Nigel M Gibbs, Oriette Stubbs, Paul Wardle, Peter Tottman, Ruralbob, Sally Catling, Sally-Anne Coton, Sim Croft (no relation), Sue (no surname), Susan Fiddes, Sylvia Crampin, Tremayne Alflatt, Tracey Clark, Claire Evans, Lisa-Marie Thompson and Tyler Porter. You're all absolute superstars.

Wow. That went on longer than I expected.

ADAM CROFT

With almost two million books sold to date, Adam Croft is one of the most successful independently published authors in the world, having sold books in over 120 different countries.

In February 2017, Amazon's overall Author Rankings briefly placed Adam as the most widely read author in the world at that moment in time, with J.K. Rowling in second place.

Adam is considered to be one of the world's leading experts on independent publishing and has been featured on BBC television, *BBC Radio 4*, *BBC Radio 5 Live*, the *BBC World Service*, *The Guardian*, *The Huffington Post*, *The Bookseller* and a number of other news and media outlets.

In March 2018, Adam was conferred as an Honorary Doctor of Arts, the highest academic qualification in the UK, by the University of Bedfordshire in recognition of his services to literature.

Adam presents the regular crime fiction podcast *Partners in Crime* with fellow bestselling author and television actor Robert Daws.

CPSIA information can be obtained
at www.ICGtesting.com
Printed in the USA
LVHW040520220720
661243LV00016B/232